The Thirsty Horse Of Mongolia

Library of Congress Catalogue in-Publication Data:

> Sansom, Anthony.
> The Thirsty Horse of Mongolia / Anthony Sansom – 1st
> Thirsty Horse LLC.

ISBN 0-9723127-0-6

Published by: Thirsty Horse LLC, 1220, North Market Street, Suite 606, Wilmington DE 19801-2598, USA.

Email: editor@thirsty-horse.com
Web Site: http//www.thirsty-horse-media.com

...

Cover Painting by D. Bold.

...

Printed in the Republic of South Korea

...

Thirsty Horse LLC,
_2003_

Acknowledgements

I would like to thank everyone who has helped, contributed, inspired or even just encouraged me along the way with the preparation of this book, and in particular all those good friends of mine who are named below:

First of all, my two fervent administrators: Mrs. Jambaa Urtnasan who organised my presentations of the project in Ulaan Baatar, and Mrs. Ayuur Enkhtsetseg who liased with my five professional artists and also translated and co-presented my speeches for me. Both of these ladies too for running the painting competition.

A very specially thank you to Ms. Michelle Oh Kyung Mi, for bringing her skills in the graphic arts to this project, and for her help and contribution throughout.

Mr. Ravdan, actor of deserved national acclaim, for making my heart glad by reading aloud from the Thirsty Horse, and thereby giving me a preview of the reaction of our audience.

The real men: Mr. Luvsandash Boldbaatar, whose tireless efforts and hard work helped me very much to discover Mongolia; and of course Zoric and Ot, who gave me that precious first adventure in the west. Herein also included, of course, Mssrs. Richard Maffioli and Lionel Pernollet from Chamonix, France, for their friendship; and for their courage and professionalism that made it possible for us to reach the highest peaks of the Altai and Khentii mountain ranges.

Mr. Brian Barnard, for his help, advice and friendship throughout.

For the quality of the writing: Ms. Kellyn Van Fossen for editing the final draft and so torturing me with her critique that I managed to improve quite markedly the difficult linguistic style of the text; and Ms. Amanda Searle from the British Council in Seoul for proof reading the result. I thank both of these ladies for their much appreciated friendship, support and excellent work.

My research assistant and very good friend Ms. Amgalan Batkhuyag who helped and inspired me always.

Finally, Mr. Damdingiin Demberel, Member of Parliament for Hovd Aimag, who has assisted us very much with his wisdom, his friendship and his support. But most of all for his vision in accepting to help us as he has.

Anthony Sansom.

Dedication

*"This is a story that belongs to us all,
for all to read and take whatever benefit they can
from its lessons of the secret of life."*

The Thirsty Horse of Mongolia

Contents

Page

Forward *by Mr. Damdingiin Demberel,*
Member of the State Great Khural (Parliament) of Mongolia,
and Chairman of the Standing Committee on State Structure   *11*

Forward *by Mrs. Ayuur Enkhtsetseg*   *12*

Author's Introduction   *15*

Part 1

In which Thirsty Horse
sets out to find the end of the steppe,
even though he knows that
no such place exists.

Chapter

1 – To the End of the Steppe   *29*

2 – The Cup of Curiosity Speaks   *39*

3 – The Sound of a River   *53*

4 – School   *65*

5 – The Town on the Edge of the Steppe   *81*

6 – Last day at School – and what
*   have you learned?*   *97*

Part 2

*In which Thirsty Horse
leaves the school on the edge of the steppe
and travels the world in search of an answer
to the question of the Cup of Curiosity,
"What is the secret of life?"*

Page

Chapter

7 - The Great Earth Beneath the Stars   113

8 – Journeys yet to Come   123

9 – Into the Realm of the Eagles   135

10 – The Great Han Khan   153

11 - The Journey Back   203

12 – The Secret of Life   217

Appendices:

1. "No Fear of Wolves"   225

2. Hovd and beyond: the author's visits to the west
   of Mongolia in May and December of 2002.   233

3. Illustrating the Thirsty Horse: a few more
   paintings from the competition.   239

List of Illustrations

Paintings from the Competition:

	Page
"Night Upon the Open Steppe." - by Batchimeg	14
"Tell me, Far Seeing Horse." - by U. Ochirsuren	27
"Thirsty Horse Chased by Wolves." - by U. Ochirsuren	28
"Thirsty Horse Enters the Ger." - by U. Ochirsuren	37
"The Cup of Curiosity." - by Enkhbayarin Psargal	38
"Thirsty Horse Becomes a Boy."	51
"Erdenbaatar teaches Music to Thirsty Horse." by Lhagvasuren Batileg	52
"To the Edge of the Steppe." by Bolortuya	63
"Night upon the Open Steppe." by Lhagvasuren Batileg	64
"Thirsty Horse escapes from the 'Kind Boys'"	79
"To the Town on the Edge of the Steppe." - by Dashdorj Uyanga	80
"Thirsty Horse and the man in the strangely coloured Robe."	95
"How to play the Guitar?" by N. Zutgel	96
"Thirsty Horse tells his Story to the class." by Ganbat Altanbagana	109
"Thirsty Horse plays Guitar upon the Open Steppe." by L. Sukhbat	110
"The Great Earth Beneath the Stars." by S. Baasanjargal	121
"Stories by Khovskul Lake." by A. Lhagvasuren	122
"Khovskol Lake." by Adilbish Javzandulam	133
"The Bear" - by B. Odbold	134
"Proclamation on the Mountain's Peak." by D. Bulganbayar	151
"Asleep Beneath the Stars upon the Open Steppe."	202
"The Great Gobi Desert." by Ganbold Boldhuyag	224

Appendix 3 paintings (clockwise from top): E. Tsolmon; B. Bat-Orshih; E. Uganbayar; Bayaraa Huyag ; last page by S. Monkhsaruul

Sketches:

"Wolves" by Enkbaatarin Ariunbayar - page 2; "Thirsty Horse the Boy" by P. Sarangerel - page 6; "Shadows" by B. Bathishig - page 10; "Thirsty Horse" by T. Ankhbayar - page 26; "Boy, be a Horse Again." by G Batmonk - page 76; "Sneaking past the School Administrator." by P. Sarangerel - page 89; "Thirsty Horse Plays Guitar." - page 112; "Khovsol Lake." - page 127; "View from the Last Peak of the Khangai Range." by Ganbold Boldhuyag - page 141; "Thirsty Horse - as Tough as the Mountains had made him." by Enkh-Amgalan Erhemsuld - page 157; "Looking Back" - page 205;

From the Professional Artists:

"In search of the Secret of Life" - by Dorjin Narantsetseg (Nara)	13
"The Challenge of the Guard" - by Dorjsurengiin Erdenebileg (Erke).	152
"Before the Great Han Khan" - by Tserendorjin Olzbaatar (Olzo).	165
"The Army of the Great Khan" - by Erke.	166
"Boy, be a horse again!" - by Nara	183
"The Spirit of Thirsty Horse"- by Yadamsurengiin Oyunchimeg (Oyuna).	184
"These are the gifts of the stars to men." - by Luvsandorjin Bavuudorj	201
"The Great Spirit of Music." - by Luvsandorjin Bavuudorj	215
"Music Maker's skill and the guitar remade." - by Oyuna.	216
"The Last Wish." - by Olzo.	223

9

Forward by Mr. Damdingiin Demberel
Member of the State Great Khural (Parliament) of Mongolia, and Chairman of the Standing Committee on State Structure

Just pick up this book. Flick through a few pages and glance at the paintings and the photographs, read a passage or two - and there! Now the spirit of Mongolia has come alive for you. Read on and you will find, as I did, that Anthony Sansom's descriptions of our vast and beautiful land are as exotic, fascinating, and magical as the characters and events that he depicts in his story.

But beware! Because this story of the Thirsty Horse of Mongolia as he travels across steppe and desert and mountain alike in search of the secret of life is not just an amusing folk tale. It is a modern legend full of great insight and depth whose eventual reach only time will reveal. And quite possibly, too, it will lead you inevitably to set out upon your own search for the secret of life before very long.

It is a story that is described at the very beginning as, "something that happened just a few years ago." Yet it seemed to me as I read it through that it has a certain timeless immediacy to it, such that I might even awake tomorrow and find it as reality in the newspapers, which would actually be rather a good thing, I believe.

Thirsty Horse is a hero who journeys across all of Mongolia paying his way by honest work and learning from his life as he goes: a character innocent enough to wonder with an open heart, yet courageous enough to ask his question of all. A boy who is led by his simple belief in destiny and innate purpose to a noble sense of values, and when finally he must, to the defiance, even, of a ruthless king. Here indeed, is a new myth for the new age.

This is a story that has much to teach us all and I think that there are many people all over the world who will take the example of the Thirsty Horse very much to their hearts. So now read on, and when you reach the end of the book - yes, then you will know the secret of life.

Forward by
Mrs. Ayuur Enkhtsetseg

I first met Anthony Sansom over a year ago as a visitor with a passionate love for Mongolia - especially the countryside and the western aimags.

At that time I was working as the External Relations Officer for the National Children's Committee and was preparing a brief narrative about the situation of children in Mongolia to present at a world summit meeting. This led us to talk about children, who are our future, and I think myself that it was that conversation that set the first spark to the inspiration for the Thirsty Horse that was already smouldering in Anthony's mind. Now, of course, the book has become reality and it is a fabulous accomplishment that has taken an awful lot of hard work. So I am very proud to have been asked, and to have been able, to assist by way of the children's competition and with the artists, in bringing to be this modern fable for the people of the 21st century. It has a lot of good ideas and will, I think, go a very long way.

As for Anthony, I think that he is himself really a thirsty horse who is looking for the secret of life. While I think he would appreciate the sentiment that I am especially proud, too, of my country. That it should have been here that he came to find it.

...

The Thirsty Horse of Mongolia

Author's Introduction

So what is the job of a writer? Is it to invent the story in its entirety, word by carefully planned word of its studied construction? Or is it nothing more than to order and present the inspiration that comes from somewhere unknown – after trying to keep up while writing it down? This question I ask myself now, and in answer cannot escape the conclusion that there was more to the writing of the Thirsty Horse than came from my mind alone. But then, perhaps the journey of the writer was ever to find his muse and to commune, which surely works best when the harmony sounds well between the two - and so it was we, I believe, who wrote this book.

Personally I thought it was a story just for children that I had set out to write, and certainly the first chapter reads well as such. But finally, I believe, it is a work that may be read with pleasure by adult and child alike, since my muse had this plan for the book - and what choice had I then but to follow suit.

So as the writing began to count the pages I saw my central character grow quickly in maturity while the story unfolded ever more profoundly before me. Until I was forced to accept the situation for what it was: to let the hero develop with the telling of his tale, and the style of the writing to evolve with it too. While I was also obliged, lest you should wonder at the end of the story, to ascribe its narration to a character within its compass rather than to myself.

The Thirsty Horse of Mongolia

The Thirsty Horse of Mongolia is very much a work of inspiration and my several muses in fact, for that is how I understand it, were the spirits of Mongolia whose paths I crossed while I travelled in that land. Of course I am far too much a westerner to claim that these spirits actually appeared before me or spoke to me in magical disembodied voices. Yet such as my experiences were, it would not be so far from the truth if I claimed even this. So saying, I would like to communicate to you, the esteemed and valued reader of this book, something of how these spirits called upon me to write it. And for this reason it is, that I have included within these pages some words and images from those episodes of my life that were most instrumental in bringing that inspiration to my mind.

...

I had visited Mongolia four times before the first muse took hold of my mind, gave it a good shake I should say too, and commenced to breathe the life of this story into me.

The first visit was in August of 2000. When I came to Ulaan Baatar and watched happy children playing by the fountain by Sukhbaatar Square; then visited the Terelj National Park, where I walked in its beautiful mountains while they were clad with the green of summer.

So impressed was I with my first visit that I came back in January of 2001, to Ulaan Baatar, and to the Terelj as well where I did some skiing. For my own pleasure I made a short film of the experience. But then since the result exceeded my expectations I sold sixty copies of it with the intention to donate all of the money to the National Committee for Children in Mongolia – the NCC.

With the money from the film in my pocket I arrived back in Ulaan Baatar, or UB as it is known locally, in May of 2002. This time I was also intending that same week to take a trip to the western region. The idea behind this was principally to research the possibility of making a much more ambitious film in the Altai Mountains, for which purpose I had selected Mount Tsambagarav (4202 m) as a test case. Unfortunately, however, this expedition would leave me with only one evening back in UB upon my return to meet with the NCC and present the money from the film.

Not speaking Mongolian, I had intended to take a guide with me from Ulaan Baatar. But in the event I decided to go alone and just take my chances. Standing in Hovd airport some hours later; however, while waiting for my luggage to arrive from the plane and looking around at all those unfamiliar faces smiling their non-communication, I really began to wonder if this trip hadn't been a mistake. I noticed too that there was no snow at all on the mountains around Hovd, which didn't sit well with my intention to make a film about skiing in this location. But things started to go my way again when by chance I met up with Zoric, who spoke a little English, in the taxi between the airport and the hotel. Then he introduced me to his friend Ot - "the demon God of four wheel drive," who obviously owned a jeep; and very soon after that the logistics for my expedition to Mount Tsambagarav had all fallen neatly into place.

Leaving me at the Buyant Hotel, the guys said they'd be back tomorrow morning early, but in the event they were only gone long enough to get petrol – an encouraging indication of their enthusiasm for the trip, I thought. So we left Hovd at 3:00 in the afternoon and headed out across the Buyant River, where the ice still piled in decks of broken slabs that showed themselves perhaps a metre thick even though the air in May was no more than cool.

The three of us spent four days in the Western Gobi Desert just north of Hovd on an expedition to the foot of my chosen mountain, and as you can see from the photographs in this book it was truly a fabulous experience. Yet for me it was far more than that, for it would reveal itself to be the culmination of all that I had seen and learned on my past visits to Mongolia. A journey that could not so much be measured in miles, but better expressed as the spiritual distance from the beautiful mountains of the Terelj National Park to the faces of the poor in Ulaan Baatar. Or in other words, now that I had followed my destiny into the depths of this land - its spirits were preparing to acknowledged my presence and reveal to me their hearts.

Now when I say that I followed my destiny, please do not imagine this to mean that I abandoned myself to my fate. For in as much as the trick of life lies in following the road of your destiny faithfully wherever it leads, it also requires that you maintain a very strict control over your speed on the journey and that you, yourself, carefully avoid the obstacles and potholes that you meet along the way. So you will appreciate from this, for instance, that I did not drink the copious quantities of vodka that were offered to me continuously during the trip, save for a very little to be polite – and that was good, I had been advised, to guard against the possibility of gastro-enteritis in any case.

For four days we travelled in Ot's jeep to and from the Altai Mountains, met the nice people of the village of Erden Boren, and slept in the gers of nomadic herdsmen along the way. Finally I climbed high enough in the foothills of Mount Tsambagarav to at least reach the snow line and take a few photographs. And I walked three times around the cairn (Ovoo in Mongolian) on the summit of my particular foothill in reverence to its spirit.

In the event I didn't climb the mountain itself, although I would certainly have liked to. But since my intention had been more reconnaissance than climbing, I at least achieved my ambition for this mission if no more.

In those four days I saw so much of the western region: its deserts and its mountains, its rivers and its lakes, its animals and its plants; and most of all its peoples. By gracious virtue of their hospitality: from the magnificence of their spirit laid bare in their open hearts, to their stoic endurance of their poverty and their pains; their simplicity, and most of all the proud courage of their independence. All the lessons of their lives laid out and presented for my review and grateful edification.

There was, too, a moment that I should tell you of which seemed very strange to me. It was on the way back from Mount Tsambagarav, when we had stopped and were discussing the mountain with people met along the way. As I have said, I did not drink the vodka that was offered on such occasions beyond a very little to be polite. Yet still I partook of the moment and the hospitality of the custom, while I listened to my friends talk and sometimes spoke a little when Zoric would interpret. Perhaps it was important too, I realise as I write this now, that I did not hurry the moment itself. But anyway, I listened and I watched: the greetings, the customs; and the discussion that I understood in part at least, from gestures certainly but from familiarity by now with the ways of the people too; and I knew that they talked of the mountain and of its spirit. So I listened, and as I did a new appreciation came to form very strongly within my mind of the mountain as not just a geographic feature, but also as a sentient entity! You will notice that I do not say here "realised," for this sentiment is something that I knew very well already. Yet suddenly it seemed real to me that the mountain was indeed a spirit when it had not seemed as such before – and it is that understanding that came newly to me then.

Now I must tell you that it rained while I travelled in the desert and I will tell you too that the mountains around Hovd were all white with snow upon my return. And to break the enigma of this news I will tell you that the rain is an omen of good fortune, or so the Mongolians say. While the snow was certainly one of good fortune to me – who came carrying his skis upon his back.

...

"Huge open spaces, grandiose communist architecture, and happy children playing in the cold," is how I summarised Mongolia in my film; and it wasn't until I was seated on the 'plane and flying back from Hovd to Ulaan Baatar that I discovered the naivete of my understanding. When finally I opened a book that I had bought a few days before and read about the great terror and the years of Stalin and Choibalsan: about the 100,000 dead in unmarked graves around Ulaan Baatar and the systematic extermination of the intelligentsia and the Buddhist Priesthood. Things that nobody ever talks about, because people are proud - and they do not say.

...

It was snowing in UB too when I got back from the western region, and the Bogd Khan Mountain that marks the southern limit of the city was blanketed again in winter white, just as the mountains around Hovd had been on the day I left. Since my plane had been delayed for one day in its departure, I had missed my connection and had three days more than I had expected to spend in Ulaan Baatar - three very useful days that I was grateful to have, that is. So I made just sufficient enquiries from the MIAT office to know for sure that they hadn't been able to arrange an alternative flight for me via Beijing. Then I went very happily on my way with my extra time at my disposal, to make the best use of it that I could.

The next day I met again with the NCC and presented to their External Relations Officer the money from the film. Then she, in return, presented me with a child's painting by way of a thank you – and that gave me yet another idea. Instead of finding a single artist to illustrate my book as I had intended, I would hold a national competition for Mongolian children and run it through all the schools in the country. Great!

In the event I developed my thinking upon this theme a little more, and while thinking I eventually returned to my initial thoughts as well. Finally it occurred to me that the illustrations for the first nine chapters of the book should be procured by way of a competition open to children and young people, but that I should commission 10 paintings from professional artists for the last three chapters. This seemed to be the solution that best respected that aspect of the book's style in that it continually evolves in complexity as the story is told - and with this reasoning I found myself content.

...

So that is how the story came to be and how I came to set up such an elaborate scheme for the procurement of the book's illustrations. But what, finally, of my muse for the Thirsty Horse of Mongolia: of the spirits who inspired me to write?

What use, even, for this book - in a country where I was once told that, "People are too poor to read books?" Unless for my reply that, "People remain poor because they don't read books." And perhaps what I really want from the Thirsty Horse is to change their way of thinking, although that does seem to be rather ambitious a goal. But then it was the spirits of Mongolia who inspired me to write this book and do not the spirits of Mongolia care for their people? I at least believe that they do.

With everything else now said, and as well as I can say it at least, I finish this introduction with my most sincere hope that all of this will be of some interest and entertainment to others as well as to myself. The story will never be heard if it is not; and then the spirits of Mongolia - my muse, will be just as disappointed as I. But on this question I have no desire to conclude nor defend myself in any way. For no conclusion of importance lies with me to make; and it is only you, the reader, who may say good or bad of this work - and thereby change the world.

Anthony Sansom.
31ˢᵗ January 2003.
Seoul, Korea

Post Script:

Now that I have had the chance to review a large part of the artwork that has been inspired by the Thirsty Horse, I note that there are many minor contradictions between this and the story. From the many children who have painted Thirsty Horse as a horse while he plays the guitar, for instance, to the collective decision of my artists to transform the guitar itself into a form of mandola, since the guitar is not a instrument known to Mongolian traditional music.

Nevertheless I must confess myself to be highly delighted with the artwork and I have happily included all of these contradictions without change, to the better wealth of the project I believe. I hope that you will agree with me that it is much more interesting to see how the Thirsty Horse has inspired the imagination of the artists, than it would have been to undertake a process of correction and rejection for the sake of mechanical precision. And anyway, the spirit of the competition as stated on the application form was always this, "Artists are encouraged to use their imaginations in the interpretation of the stated themes and need not be bound by a strict interpretation so long as the basic principles of illustrating the story and its setting are respected."

In conclusion, "Thirsty Horse" developed naturally into a collaboration between myself and my muse, as writer, and the Mongolian people as artists. I am immensely proud of the response that I have received from my fellow collaborators, and just as proud of the equality of respect for each other's art that has resulted too.

A note on the Great Han Khan:

Now here I should include a note about the character of The Great Han Khan, who appears very prominently within the story. Mongolians will assume that this character is based upon their greatest hero, Genghis Khan, which I know for a fact because several of them have already told me as much. It is therefore important to know that this is not the case at all. Certainly the Great Han Khan himself would have been inspired by the legend and majesty of Genghis Khan - for who indeed is not. Yet the character that I have cast is of a very different mould indeed: a man of much smaller spirit and notable lack of vision, who finds himself as an anachronistic warlord dreaming uncertainly of a domination and conquest that are not within his destiny or his times. In truth I still like my character, the Great Han Khan, for he has courage in his place at least, and he has a certain style. Yet his mind is too small for him to look up humbly to the stars and ask, "Tell me all." For he is frightened that he will lose himself in the ocean of their knowledge and their wisdom; which of course marks the difference between the Great Han Khan and Thirsty Horse.

So finally the Great Han Khan is not based on Genghis Khan. Yet the character is loosely inspired by another man much closer to his own character: a man of similar strength and lack of vision; although as to whom that may be, specifically, I will leave it to you, the reader, to discern.

One last note on language with regard to the Great Han Khan, which I include to counter in advance the inevitable complaints of inconsistency in the text. "Khan," as most will be aware, means "King." Hence in the forms of address employed, "Oh Great Han Khan," would correspond to "Oh Great King Han " While "Oh Great Khan," simply, "Oh Great King. Such a long title as "The Great Han Khan the Magnificent, Lord of the Eternal Horde, King of all the Mongols and Emperor of all the World" becomes tedious to repeat at full length. So I found it natural, therefore, for his subjects to seek variation in the form of address, even in part to avoid boring the King with the long repetition of the full title. While since the shorter the form used, the more one would risk offending the Great Khan, the abbreviation also assimilates a deeper and deeper ingratiation the shorter it becomes. Interestingly, one discerns a whole interplay of social positioning taking place within the employment of the term of address.

And finally, concerning the competition:

So many excellent paintings were received that is a pity not to have been able to include more of them in the book. My gratitude to all who entered, and the winners were as follows:

1st prize overall went to B. Odbold (18)
2nd prizes were awarded to: L. Sukhbat (15), and E. Tsolmon (8)
3rd prizes: N. Zutgel (14), B. Bat-Orshih (180), Lhagvasuren (16), B. Uugansamai, B. Shijir (10), A. Sainbileg (11), B. Anhbayar (13), N. Tuul (18).
4th prizes: U. Ochirsuren (9), B. Olziibat (12), Sh. Sarangerel (13), D. Uyanga (13), Ch. Lutsukh (13), E. Jargal (10), J. Bolathan (10), G. Batmonkh (12), O. Tsend-Ayush (14), S. Baasanjargal (15).

Anthony Sansom.
9th May, 2003.
Seoul, Korea

Part 1

*In which
Thirsty Horse sets out
to find the end of the steppe,
even though he knows
that no such place
exists.*

Chapter 1:
To the End of the Steppe

Mongolia is a vast and open country of mountains and desert but mostly steppe, which is where the grass grows well but the trees are very few. For on the steppe it does not rain enough for such big plants as those.

With all this grass to eat and all this land you could run so far upon the steppe, or so they say, that your ears would grow tired of the sound of your own hoof beats before you reached its end. Although what they mean by this, of course, is that you would never reach its end. For to grow tired of the beat of your hooves, they say as well, is to grow tired of the beat of your heart. They are the horses who live there, for it is a land that the horses call their own. There are men too, of course, and there are even towns. But the horses believe that mostly the land is theirs, and that there are many more horses than there are men, which is true.

This is the story of one of these horses, and it is not an old traditional story, although I think that it will be one day; and since I do believe this I have written it down in a style that will suit such recognition when it arrives. But even so, for now it is something that happened just a very few years ago.

Now this horse, who was quite a young horse, could gallop further and faster than any other horse of his own age, and he looked the part. For you might say, if you saw him, that he could run so well because he had such good strong legs and such a fine athletic body to achieve it with, and that is partly true. But the real reason why he ran so fast was simply because it was his heart's desire so to do, and his fine athletic body and good strong legs were really no more than a consequence of his heart's desire. Since he galloped so fast he was always the first to drink at the river; and since he galloped so much he seemed always to be drinking the water of the river, which in fact he was. In fact so very often was he thirsty from this exercise of his heart's desire that that is how he had earned his name. For his name was Thirsty Horse.

...

The story begins on one beautiful summer's day when all was still and calm in the warm air and the herd was grazing quietly by the river. Or perhaps it would be more correct to say that the story begins, although at the same moment, with the sound of hoof beats galloping at great speed from the open steppe. Since the gallop was so fast and only the hooves of one horse could be heard, there was no doubt amongst the other horses as to who this could be - as Thirsty Horse came thundering towards the herd and shuddered to a stop by the river, there to cool himself for a moment before he drank.

There was nothing unusual in this, of course, except that today Thirsty Horse had something on his mind. So once he had drunk enough from the river he cantered up to the wisest horse of the herd, whose name was Far Seeing Horse, and he asked, "Please tell me, Far Seeing Horse, where is the end of the steppe?"

"That is easy, Thirsty Horse," replied the other without even looking up from his grazing, "for the steppe never ends, as you know."

"Yes, you are right, Far Seeing Horse." sighed Thirsty Horse in agreement. "For in fact I know this very well." But then he tossed his head and reared upon his hind legs as he neighed in his exasperation, "And yet there is something in my mind which says that it isn't so!" Then Thirsty Horse thought for a moment before he asked, "Please tell me, Far Seeing Horse, for today this something is tormenting me very much. I do not doubt that your knowledge is true - but what must I do to know it for myself?"

Then Far Seeing Horse replied, "A lot of trouble you will give yourself for nothing, Thirsty Horse. Yet since you like to run so much you may prove to yourself, if you wish, that what is true is true." Then Far Seeing Horse looked up from his grazing and said, "You see that solitary tree over there so very far away?"

Thirsty Horse looked – and looked, and finally he could just make out the tree. For Far Seeing Horse could, indeed, see very, very far, and it really was a very long way away.

"Yes," he confirmed, "I can see it."

"That tree is called As Far as We Can See." explained Far Seeing Horse. "Yet if you gallop as far as that tree and then look beyond it, still you will find that the steppe continues for as far as you can see again! By that, Thirsty Horse, you will know that the steppe never ends. If you wish to prove it then you must gallop all day from that tree to the next mark that you can see, and then to the next and the next and so on. All day in the same direction without ever stopping or even so much as looking back you must gallop, and you will find that the steppe is just the same no matter how far you go. That you may do if you wish, Thirsty Horse, and perhaps you will, for I see that in your heart there is still doubt. But if you do, then take care. For there are wolves upon the open steppe and very quickly you will be much too far from the herd for any of us to help you."

Now it seemed to Thirsty Horse that the wisdom of Far Seeing Horse was correct. Yet for some strange reason, and as Far Seeing Horse had so clearly understood, still his heart was not content to believe it. So he drank once more from the river, and then he set off at a steady pace that he judged to be fast enough to reach the tree called As Far as We Can See but not so fast as to tire him out before he got there.

As he left, Far Seeing Horse stopped his grazing once more and lifted his head to watch Thirsty Horse as he galloped off into the distance. "Good Luck Thirsty Horse," he said, "and good bye young friend. You must follow your heart for your heart is tormented and that may take you further than even I can see. Into the bellies of the wolves, most probably. But perhaps to somewhere beyond the knowledge of the horses that I do not know. If such a place exists, then I hope it is there that you go. But whatever happens, this day will be long for you, young friend, for you are driven by the force of your destiny, and days such as those are very long indeed."

Actually it was only about an hour later when Thirsty Horse reached the tree, and he had not yet even begun to feel tired. He stopped by the tree, and he looked beyond it, and he saw that the words of Far Seeing Horse were indeed correct. For the steppe did continue just the same as before and for as far as he could see again!

For quite a while Thirsty Horse stood still by the tree and considered what to do next, now that he had reached As Far as We Can See; and he considered very carefully indeed for it was a very serious matter to go beyond this point. But then all of a sudden he made up his mind and he set off again, in the same direction and at the same gallop, for that was his heart's desire.

For many hours Thirsty Horse galloped on until even his steady pace began to slow, while still the unchanging steppe unrolled like an endless carpet of green before him. Yet Thirsty Horse continued on his way without so much as a pause to recover his strength. For whether he knew it yet or not, the great journey of his life had now begun.

Thirsty Horse was still galloping steadily on by the time the sun dipped low in the sky and he knew that the night was just an hour away. He thought to stop, for now he really was tired, but the steppe continued on and on the same, just as before, and there was nowhere for him to stop. He realised too that he had come much too far to go back to the herd, and yet still he had gone nowhere! The steppe did indeed go on forever - and it was then that he finally grew afraid. While as bad luck would have it his fear was very soon justified too. For it was at that exact moment that he heard from behind him the first howl of a wolf!

Tired or not there was no choice now but to gallop, and to gallop as fast as he could away from the wolves and so that is what Thirsty Horse did. While he galloped, he heard the howls of the wolves coming louder and closer from behind him and to both sides of him as well. But he galloped on as fast as he could and he simply ignored the tiredness in his legs and the straining of his lungs for air. He ran so fast that soon the sounds of the wolves did not come any closer and he knew that if only he could keep going at this speed for long enough he would outrun them and escape. But then suddenly there appeared immediately before him two huge and savage wolves with flashing fangs menacing in their open mouths as they raced towards him, and he realised that he had been caught in a trap!

Now the sight of these two huge wolves snarling and slavering before him was enough to make Thirsty Horse think very quickly indeed. And what he thought so very quickly was that there was only one thing that he could do to escape. So he summoned all the strength that remained to him, however tired he was, and he jumped as high into the air as he possibly could. Then so high did he jump that it was almost as if he flew. And although he did feel the teeth of one of the wolves as it bit him, it was only against the hard horn of his hoof that the animal bit, which was worse for the wolf than it was for the horse.

When Thirsty Horse landed from his jump he galloped still for all he was worth and even faster than before, for his fear spurred him on. Then the howls of the wolves receded behind him and he knew that

33

this time he really had escaped. "Or at least," he thought, "for now." For he knew that the wolves were tracking him and would catch him yet when he stopped – unless, of course, he could gallop all the way to the end of the steppe before they did? So with that thought in his mind, Thirsty Horse continued to gallop as fast as he could, still without stopping or ever slowing down.

So Thirsty Horse galloped for the end of the steppe to save his life; and all the while he galloped, the words of Far Seeing Horse were ringing ever true in his mind, "A lot of trouble you will give yourself for nothing, Thirsty Horse. Yet since you like to run so much you may prove to yourself, if you wish, that what is true is true. For the steppe never ends, as you know."

It was, indeed, a difficult situation, and Thirsty Horse was becoming very, very tired. Indeed so tired was he becoming that no one would ever have blamed him if he had simply stopped in his exhaustion, and feeling sorry for himself accepted his fate. But he didn't, and the reason why he didn't was simply because there was no place in his heart where any such despair could be found. While what he thought instead was that if he would die by the teeth of the wolves then at least he would run as far and as fast as any horse had ever run before and that would be his life's accomplishment – before they ate him! So on and on he galloped towards the great white ball of the sun as it set; and all the while he ran he saw nothing save the brilliance of its glow in the distance and by its light the ground just before his feet.

While Thirsty Horse ran on to his life's accomplishment the sun sank lower and lower in the sky - until suddenly it was gone and he had to stop, for it was dark. Then in the darkness he looked around him for the first time since he had heard the first wolf howl, and he wondered where he was. It was very quiet and there were no howls from wolves to be heard now. For although they tracked him certainly, they were a very long way behind.

Without the setting sun to blind him anymore his eyes adjusted to the light of the full moon, which shone very brightly in the night sky, and so he could see at least a little way before him. He stood still for a moment, and he looked around, and he listened too - and then he heard a noise! But it was not a noise that frightened him, and certainly it was not a wolf. For it was, in fact, the bleating of a goat! In great surprise Thirsty Horse cantered forward towards the sound of the goat, and then to his delight he saw, in dark silhouette against the moonlight, several of the Big Round Things Upon the Ground with Smoke Coming out of the Tops of Them" that he knew to be the homes of men. Then Thirsty Horse knew that here was a place that the wolves would fear, and although he had not reached the end of the steppe, it was still a very good place to be.

The next thing that Thirsty Horse discovered was something that smelt of wood but looked very unnatural indeed; and so although he had never seen its like before, he knew that this too had been made by men. By the light of the moon he made it out to be a square enclosure, and it was inside this enclosure that he found the goats. Then he saw that the goats were drinking from an extremely small pool of water inside their enclosure – and he suddenly realised how very thirsty he was himself. His immediate thought was to drink from the goats' pool, but he could not reach it from outside and the idea of jumping over the fence to get inside made him realise how tired he was. Yet that is what he decided to do, since he really had no other choice, and since he knew that he would need a good long run to get up enough speed for the jump he cantered off a fair distance for this purpose.

Before he had gone quite far enough, however, he heard another sound – and it was a sound so beautiful and so familiar that it made his heart leap with happiness. Because it was undoubtedly the sound of water trickling across a stone in a river! And yet it was a strange sound too, for it was not quite right somehow? But it was the sound of water, nevertheless, and it was coming from the inside of one of the Big Round Things Upon the Ground with Smoke Coming out of its Top that the men lived in.

Cautiously, Thirsty Horse approached the Big Round Thing Upon the Ground with Smoke Coming out of its Top that had the sound of strange water coming from within. Then three times he walked all the way around it - but he could not find any way in!

All there was to give him any clue to an entrance was a rectangular shape in the side that appeared as if it would move if he pushed it and then leave an opening just big enough for him to squeeze through. So Thirsty Horse pushed at the shape with his nose a few times, and each time he pushed it moved a little but still stayed firmly in place. While all the time the sound of the water from inside was tantalising him so much and his thirst was growing so much worse - until finally he could stand it no more! So he reared up on his hind legs and smashed the shape to pieces with one tremendous blow from his hooves – and then, perhaps just a little shyly I may say, he lowered his head – and looked inside.

...

Chapter 2:
The Cup of Curiosity Speaks

Thirsty Horse stepped cautiously over the remains of the door that he had just smashed to pieces and then with an effort squeezed himself carefully through the narrow opening. It was fortunate that he was not yet quite fully-grown, he thought to himself, or he would not have been able to get in at all.

Once inside he looked around with cautious inquisitiveness and found that he was indeed in a strange world full of many strange things that he had never seen before. And not only were there strange things inside the Big Round Thing upon the Ground with Smoke Coming out of its Top - but there were men inside too! Now Thirsty Horse himself had only seen men a very few times before, but he had heard many tales of them and their peculiar ways from the other horses. So he knew only too well that men are the most mysterious and unpredictable of all the animals that live upon the steppe and it would have been quite understandable for him to have become a little bit scared in his present, unusual situation. Indeed he probably would have been scared, had it not been for one special feature of this moment that struck him as so very strange as to distract his mind away from his fear. And what it was that so took Thirsty Horse's attention was that all the men, who were now looking at him so very intently, were completely silent! Because never in all his life had he ever known, or even so much as heard tell in fact, of men without the endless sound of their peculiar neighing and whinnying being there to accompany them!

It was a shock indeed, and for quite a few seconds Thirsty Horse was really just too stunned to react at all. But then suddenly he realised the reason for their silence, "Of course!" he thought to himself, "How could it not be so." For it was obvious that the men had been trapped inside the Big Round Thing upon the Ground with Smoke Coming out of its Top, and with their small and weak bodies had not been able to escape. Once he realised that he had, in fact, just saved them all from slowly starving to death, he could easily understand their silence and the reverent attention they paid him now. Being really quite a modest character, however, he did no more than to acknowledge their gratitude with a polite snort from his nostrils, and then he continued to look around for the water.

Now it is another strange feature of men that they are very seldom found standing up, and when they are not going anywhere - never! So once he got over the shock of their silence, Thirsty Horse was not in the least surprised to see that the men had arranged a very interesting display of the most peculiar constructions in order to accommodate their habits of reclining. There were even a number of what looked like extraordinarily flat stones, although they were made of wood according to Thirsty Horse's sense of smell. Upon these the men had placed their food - and there indeed was another strange wonder, although to Thirsty Horse a rather pointless one. Since whatever plants it was that they ate, surely this wonder would serve no other purpose than to deny the men the freshness of those plants as they grew from the ground? But then, he thought to himself too, perhaps this was not actually their usual behaviour. For perhaps the men had done this just to pass the time while they had considered themselves to be locked for the rest of their days within the Big Round Thing upon the Ground with Smoke Coming out its Top.

But whatever: now that he was inside, Thirsty Horse's real concern was for the river that he had heard and which, since the place was really quite small, must surely now be right before his nose. Indeed, surely it must be? Yet no matter how hard he looked to find it, there was no river to be seen! While what was even more disturbing, was that the sound of its water trickling across a stone had stopped as well; which left Thirsty Horse feeling particularly surprised since he knew very well that it is not at all the usual behaviour of a river to stop its flow so suddenly. Rivers were usually very consistent in their ways and only changed slowly with the seasons, he recalled to reassure himself on this point.

"What have the men done?" the thought crossed his mind. But whatever they had done, and wherever the river had gone, there was still the faint smell of water that lingered upon the air at least. So considering himself to be just a little bit too clever for the men and their tricks, Thirsty Horse continued his search for the water, wherever it may be, and by his sense of smell sure enough he did find it.

But then what a disappointment that was! For rather than the plentiful supply of a flowing stream that he had expected, there was no more water than was contained in what looked like a very large hollowed out nut that stood alone upon one of the extraordinarily flat wooden stones. "Really this is very little water at all!" thought Thirsty Horse to himself as the pleasure of his anticipation slowly died within him.

Yet even that was not the only problem. For the nut was even too small for Thirsty Horse to get his nose into and he knew, for he was in fact quite clever for a horse, that if he tried too hard to do so he would upset the nut. Then all the water would spill out upon the ground and be lost, for that is the way of water as Thirsty Horse had understood from the very first rain that he had ever seen fall.

Still the problem had to be solved, though - and quickly. Because Thirsty Horse was as thirsty now as would justify his name all over again. So he approached the nut; and he stiffed carefully at the water that it contained. He thought for a while, and then he nudged the nut very gently with his nose and saw that it moved, which confirmed his fears that the water could easily be spilled and lost. So what to do? – And then Thirsty Horse had an idea! He gripped the nut firmly in his teeth and in one swift movement tossed back his head so that the water drained into his mouth, which seemed rather to prove that his idea had been a good one. And indeed it had been a good idea – but only for as far as it went. For what Thirsty Horse had not realised was that even though he now had the water in his mouth, he could not swallow it all the while that he held the nut in his teeth as well. What's more, neither could he lower his head to put the nut down again without the water running out of his mouth and quite possibly being lost.

It seemed that in solving the problem Thirsty Horse had created a dilemma. But then even a dilemma can be solved if one tries hard enough to solve it. For it is no more really than a problem by another name; and that is simply to say that more thought was required. So Thirsty Horse thought about the dilemma for several seconds more - before he had another idea that was just as good as the first. Then with his head still tilted back and his eyes focused mostly upon the ceiling, he relaxed the grip of his teeth on the nut, while he tossed his head very lightly from side to side, and lo and behold the nut fell from his mouth to the floor. Then Thirsty Horse gratefully drank down all the water in one swift gulp and let out a great sigh of happiness, feeling his thirst to be far more satisfied than he had expected. And not only that, of course, but he also felt very pleased with himself for having been so clever.

Now: having solved first the problem, then the dilemma, and eventually having drunk down all the water without spilling a drop, Thirsty Horse would have been quite content to forget all about the nut episode and continue on his way. As for the nut, however - the nut had other ideas, and no intention of forgetting about Thirsty Horse. – Oh no! No! The nut had another plan entirely.

In accordance with its plan, the nut rolled about on the floor for a short while until it came to rest by the feet of one of the men, who then picked it up and saw that there was writing on it; and the writing on the nut was this,

> "To whomsoever drinks from this cup – beware!
> For though the thirst of your body will surely be quenched by the water within,
> The thirst of your mind shall just as surely be awakened.
> Then you shall not rest until that thirst, too, has been quenched."

Under this evocation was written, even more surprisingly, "Now put the cup on the table in front of the horse." So that is what the man did.

Then just as Thirsty Horse was beginning to wonder what he should do next he heard, to his immense surprise, a voice that he understood - for it spoke in the language of the horses!

"Who is it who drinks from the Cup of Curiosity? Speak and tell me your name." is what the voice said; and which was enough to startle Thirsty Horse almost out of his skin! For where in this strange place could there possibly be hiding another horse? Could it be that Far Seeing Horse had set out to follow him to the end of the steppe? If so, and he was here now, then where was he? Faced with very few possibilities, Thirsty Horse made his way back to the smashed door and peered out – but there was no other horse outside!

While he looked, however, there came from behind him the peculiar sound of someone clearing his throat in a very loud and obvious fashion. Then the voice came again, this time rather more loudly, and with a somewhat more obvious note of impatience added to its timbre. "Hmm!" began the voice. "Now for the second time of asking, who is it who drinks from the Cup of Curiosity? Speak and tell me your name."

This time Thirsty Horse could not doubt that the voice came from within the Big Round Thing upon the Ground with Smoke Coming out of its Top, although for the life of him he still had no idea who had spoken. So puzzled was he, in fact, that he even looked questioningly from face to face at all the men there. But they all sat so quiet and still that they seemed to be in the grip of some strange form of hypnosis! While it was, in any case, plainly ridiculous to even imagine that any one of them could have spoken in the language of the horses! Thirsty Horse dismissed the thought, but then he had simply no idea at all who had spoken; and so finally he had no choice but to ask into the empty space and the air before him, "Who is it who is speaking to me?"

"Ah!" He heard the voice reply with really quite magnificent exasperation. "It is me! Can you not see me standing clearly before you?"

Well, Thirsty Horse looked here, and he looked there, and he looked all around. But still all he could offer in reply was a very honest, "No!"

"Then look a little lower, fool of a horse," came the voice again, "and you will see me. For I am the Cup of Curiosity."

Now Thirsty Horse, as has already been said, didn't know what a cup was. Yet he dutifully looked anyway, and then he replied, "I am sorry voice, but I do not know what a cup is, and all I can see before me – is a sort of a large nut."

There was a brief silence then before the voice spoke again. But when it did speak it was in a fashion that rather impressed Thirsty Horse with its fine and proud manner, although perhaps a little too much so really, he thought as well.

"Your eyes are looking in the right place, horse." came the voice. "However, I am not – a nut. Actually, I am the Cup of Curiosity, if you don't mind."

Then Thirsty Horse, having finally understood to whom he was speaking, replied politely but without really understanding why it was asked of him, "No – of course I don't mind. Not at all."

For no reason that was even remotely apparent to Thirsty Horse, the voice let out a very deep sigh at this. But then it settled down to a more relaxed tone and said, "Now horse, I will explain. I am the Cup of Curiosity and you have just drunk from me. So now you must fulfil the verse that is written upon me." Then the cup repeated the verse for the sake of Thirsty Horse, who obviously could not read. "To whomsoever drinks from this cup – beware! For though the thirst of your body will surely be quenched by the water within, the thirst of your mind shall just as surely be awakened. Then you shall not rest until that thirst, too, has been quenched."

"Hmm?" said Thirsty Horse thoughtfully after he heard this. "You know – err, Cup, it sounds very much to me that that is exactly the thought that was in my mind this morning when I left the herd to search for the end of the steppe - and nothing to do with drinking from the Cup of Curiosity at all."

"Ah! – But it is." replied the cup in a voice that sounded very wise indeed. "For how very true it is that the reward of discovery is given only to those who seek."

"Hmm?" said Thirsty Horse again – but then he could not quite think of a suitable response. So he asked instead, "Then is this, indeed, the end of the steppe that I have reached?"

"No." replied the cup nonchalantly. "No it is not. But you have reached an important point in your journey, nevertheless, and from here you may continue with your search if you wish - and if you wish I will help you. But first, horse, you should consider carefully whether you really wish to continue. For has not the journey so far been hard enough, and what worse perils may await you if you travel even further from your river and your herd. Consider carefully, horse, before you confirm that you wish to continue with your quest for the end of the steppe. Then if you do not, it would be better that I release you here and now from my spell."

Now when Thirsty Horse heard this he cried, "No! No! No! Please do not do that, Cup. For my dearest wish is to run all the way to the end of the steppe and to know what is there."

"Good." said the cup with a truly insensitive indifference that seemed to indicate a total lack of surprise at the answer that Thirsty Horse had given, and which was in fact the case. For it should be remembered here that the Cup of Curiosity was in fact a magic cup, and as such was possessed of really quite remarkable powers of intuition.

"Now," continued the cup, "to reach the end of the steppe is not so difficult as you might think, horse. While as for what is there, that I can tell you now: the end of the steppe is the end of the world of the horses and the beginning of the world of men.

"So, horse," continued the Cup of Curiosity, "That is what is there. But do you know what that is?"

Then Thirsty Horse thought for a while, and he thought for a while, and he thought for a while more; until he realised that once again he could not quite think of a suitable answer to give. So he replied, almost humbly, "No Cup, I do not know. For the world of men means nothing to me."

"Precisely!" said the cup. "And that is the problem." Then the cup paused to give Thirsty Horse a little time to think about this new problem, before it continued, "Now listen to me carefully, horse. If you wish to go and see the end of the steppe and then come back having not understood what you have seen at all, then go now with my blessing and I will show you the way - but I shall release you from my spell before you go. If, however, what you really wish is to know what is there, by which I mean to understand it, then you will not be able to go as a horse and you must accept that I will make of you a man. It may be either way, horse. But whichever way it is, that is something that you must decide for yourself."

Now when Thirsty Horse heard these words, he knew that he had to think very carefully before he could reply - and that took a while to do. All the while he thought the cup neither helped him, nor hindered him, nor hurried him. Until eventually Thirsty Horse replied, "Cup, my greatest pleasure in life is to run. Yet men cannot run as the horses can, and it would be a sad loss for me indeed, if I could never run as a horse again."

"That is true," replied the cup, "although in fact you would still be able to run quite fast as a man. But never so fast again as you can now that you are a horse, and I must tell you truthfully that that is the price you will have to pay, should you decide to become a man."

Then Thirsty Horse thought for a long, long while more before he replied; and when he replied it was in a voice that was very sad indeed, "If that is the price that I must pay, Cup, to know what lies beyond the steppe. Then that is the price that I must pay. For my heart tells me that it will not rest until I know."

"Good." said the cup, again matter of factly, but not quite so matter of factly this time as before. "Then as that is your decision, horse, I will give you your chance. Now listen to me carefully while I explain." and then the Cup of Curiosity explained the details of the contract that it had in mind to turn Thirsty Horse into a man and send him on his quest for the end of the steppe.

"For five years, horse," the cup began, "I will make of you a foal of men, which is called a boy. As a boy you will be able to travel to the end of the steppe and beyond it into the world of men. Once you are there you may live amongst them and you may learn from them what they know, which is actually what you seek.

"To help you during this time," continued the cup, "I will give you two gifts, which it seems to me only fair that you should have.

"First: five times you may become a horse again if you have need. You should remember that this is once for each year that you will have as a boy, although you may use these wishes all at once, or not at all, or whenever you want. To use the spell you should say, 'Boy, be a horse again,' and to undo it, 'Horse, be a boy again.'

"Second: I will give you the speech of men so that you will not have to learn it for yourself. For in their age, corresponding to your age now as a horse, you will be thirteen years old; and at that age it would be expected of you that you would be able to talk.

"These are my gifts." said the cup. "But now listen very carefully, horse, for there is one more thing for you to know." Then the cup continued, "In this time as a boy you may quench the thirst that troubles your mind. But I have a question for you, and at the end of these five years you must come back to this same place again and answer my question. If your answer is correct, and if you so wish, then you may change from a boy into a man. If your answer is wrong, however, then I shall turn you once again into a horse – and that will be that.

"Now do you accept the terms, horse?"

"Yes." said Thirsty Horse with no hesitation at all, nor even asking of the cup what its question was, for in his heart he was convinced of his decision. "Yes. I accept the terms."

"Good." said the cup. "Then from this moment on, horse, you are a boy. In five years time from this day we will meet again here in this same place, and you must answer my question, which is this; and then the cup asked,

"What is the secret of life?"

Once the question was asked the cup fell silent and spoke no more. While Thirsty Horse felt that he had been released from a spell and did not expect that it would.

Not only Thirsty Horse, though, but also the men in the Big Round Thing upon the Ground with Smoke Coming out of its Top seemed suddenly to have been released from the spell that had held them transfixed in silent attention through all that had just past; and of course as is the way with men, one of them spoke immediately. "I'll tell you the secret of life." he said. "Nothing's for free – that's the secret of life. And I've never seen a clearer demonstration of it either."

"Well, thank you very much!" said Thirsty Horse in surprise; and as he spoke now for the first time in the language of men his voice sounded very strange to his ears. But he noted the answer carefully just the same.

To be honest he was a little disappointed that he should have found the secret of life quite so quickly and easily as this. "But never mind." he thought to himself, for he would have many other things to see and to learn during the five years of his time as a boy.

...

Chapter 3:
The Sound of a River

Now that Thirsty Horse had concluded his contract with the Cup of Curiosity, and since he had already discovered the secret of life, he was rather curious to know what had happened to the river. Because even though he had found and drunk the water in the cup, he remembered very well the sound of the water running across the stone and he could not believe that there was not some explanation here somewhere for the sound itself.

Inquisitively he looked around for the source of the sound, but saw nothing that could possibly have made it. There was no tinkling stream, in fact quite clearly no running water at all, and when he thought about it neither was there really anywhere for it to run. So what was there that could possibly have made such a sound?

Thirsty Horse continued to search and to find nothing, which finally confirmed his conclusion that whatever it was that had made the sound it could not have been a river. But then he remembered that the sound had been a bit strange anyway and he wondered if, perhaps, it had been made by something outside of his experience all together? Following this thought he looked around the inside of the Big Round Thing upon the Ground with Smoke coming out of its Top once again. This time, however, he looked around with the experienced eye of one who was at least a little bit familiar with the general run of strange objects; and that was why he noticed, this time, that there was, indeed, one particularly strange object that was even more strange than all the others.

The particularly strange object was a square box made of wood. It had a long neck with the image of a horse's head carved on the end of it, and along this neck two long strings were stretched taught. There was no clue at all as to the nature of the strange object - but there was a man holding it; and since Thirsty Horse knew that men were capable of many strange and unusual things, this alone was enough to make him suspicious.

Now in order to find out if his suspicions were correct, Thirsty Horse would have to ask the man holding the strange object what it was. So taking this opportunity to use for the first time his newly given ability to speak in the language of men, that is what he did. "Excuse me, man with the strange object that is more strange than all the other strange objects," he asked, "but before I came into this Big Round Thing upon the Ground with Smoke Coming out of its Top, I heard the sound of water trickling across a stone in a river. Of course I see now that there is no river here. But something must have made the sound of it and I am suspicious that it was the strange object that you are holding." Then as it seemed to him that it would be a good idea so to do, he added, "Was it?"

Of course, this conversation did prove that the Cup of Curiosity had kept its promise and that Thirsty Horse had indeed been granted the language of men. Yet no one would have been so kind as to say that he had progressed very far with his new ability - he could well use an additional noun or two for instance. For in fact he still spoke in the manner of the horses and they do not make words for things from the world of men, preferring instead to make long descriptions based upon the things that they know themselves. But nevertheless, Thirsty Horse spoke with the clear confidence of one too naïve to know his own foolishness, and so the man holding the particularly strange object understood what Thirsty Horse had said, and even smiled to himself at the unintentional poetry of his words.

"Well, that is a very unusual question that you ask, horse!" the man replied, "yet I think that the answer is probably yes. Because this is a morin khuur, which is an instrument of music, and it does indeed make sound. But I tell you what. I will play it for you a while, if you like, and then you can tell me if it makes the sound of the water that you heard."

"Thank you." said Thirsty Horse sincerely, since he recognised the kindness of the man's offer. Then he listened, and he watched too, as the man began to play.

Now in all his life Thirsty Horse had never heard the sound of music before this day, and he realised immediately that although it reminded him of the sound of water running across a stone in a river, it was really not the same thing at all! The more he listened, the more fascinated he became, yet the less he understood it - until he really did not know what to make of it at all, except that he knew that he liked it. While he listened he watched too the man's hands and the speed with which his fingers moved upon the strings of the instrument – and he was amazed! For here, truly, was a miracle of movement far beyond the dreams of any horse with hooves.

The man did not play for long, and when he stopped he asked Thirsty Horse, "Did you like my music?"

"Yes." replied Thirsty Horse. "I liked it very much, and now I know it too for the sound that I heard. For it sounded very much like water running across a stone in a river, and yet it did not – being rather strange at the same time. But certainly that was it - and you gave it a name too – music? I think that is what you called it."

"Music indeed!" replied the man, and for some reason that Thirsty Horse did not quite understand his face took on a look of the most satisfied delight as he spoke. Then the man asked, "So horse, you liked my music. But tell me now, what did it mean to you?"

Now this was a strange question indeed and Thirsty Horse needed quite a moment to think before he could reply. Then he said, "When first I heard it I thought there was a river nearby and that I could drink from the river, so that is what it meant to me. But now that I know the strange sound for 'music' and not a river – well, now I have no idea at all what it means."

"Oh!" said the man, and it seemed to Thirsty Horse that he looked rather disappointed by this answer, which was really rather strange coming so soon after his equally inexplicable look of delight of only a few seconds ago. Men, thought Thirsty Horse to himself, certainly were strange and peculiar animals indeed – but then everybody knew that anyway. As for the man in question, though, he quickly recovered his composure and said, "Very well, horse. I see that you are completely honest in what you say - and that, of course, may be more or less complimentary for being the simple truth. But now I think that we have some work to do here, and I will help you if you like."

"Yes, yes." replied Thirsty Horse quickly, although he had no idea what the man was referring to. But he had drunk from the Cup of Curiosity and so he wished to know.

"Then I will tell you," continued the man, "that the music speaks to your heart; and now you must tell me what the music says to your heart?"

Well, this was all rather confusing to Thirsty Horse. He thought for a while, and in truth he tried very hard to understand what it was that the music had said to his heart. But finally all he could do was to repeat in his bewilderment, "I am sorry, man, but it does not mean anything to me at all."

Thirsty Horse felt rather sorry for the man when he said this, because he thought that the man would again be upset by his lack of understanding of the music. But in fact the man only sighed softly to himself before he said. "Then let us think of it another way, horse. Now, when you first heard the sound of the music and you thought that it was a river, how did you feel about that?

"Oh, very happy indeed." replied Thirsty Horse with no hesitation at all. "For I was very thirsty and the sound told me that I could drink."

"Ah! – Very good." said the man. "So you felt happy to hear the sound of the water. But sad, I imagine, that you did not find the river. Now, horse, think back to when you first came in here. You came in looking for the river and you did not find it. But instead you found the water in the cup and when you had drunk that you were not thirsty any more. Yet once you had drunk, still you wished to find the river. Now, was that not because you missed the river itself even though you had no need any more to drink?"

Thirsty Horse thought about this for a moment, and then he replied, "Yes. That is very true. For it was indeed the river itself that I missed."

"Well then." replied the man. "When music speaks to your heart it may tell you of the river that you miss or of many things that at this moment you do not have. And when the music speaks of these things that you miss it may tell you in a way that is either happy or sad, or melancholy perhaps, or in some other way depending upon its mood. That is music, horse, and that is what it says to your heart. Then the man added, "Now tell me: what did the music say to your heart this time? Was it happy; or did it tell your heart that it was sad?"

Again Thirsty Horse had to think for a moment before he could answer the question. But then suddenly he seemed to understand what the man was trying to say. So he replied, "It seemed to me, man, that the music spoke of the river that I did not find, and it seemed to me that it was," and then he hesitated for his confidence before - "sad." he committed himself to his answer.

"Yes." said the man, with a note of almost gleeful satisfaction in his voice. "You are right that the music was sad, and it was sad because it spoke of the river that you miss in your heart. But music is not magic, horse. It is only another language and one that you may understand. So I can tell you that in order to express that sadness, this music was played in a minor key.'"

"Ah!" said Thirsty Horse as if he actually understood. "I see. A minor key, eh!"

Then the man smiled again, for he had teased Thirsty Horse by telling him this fact that he knew he could not possibly understand. Yet it was not for mischief that the man had teased him, for then he said, and in a very gentle voice indeed, "Horse, it has been said many times in history that musicians are fools and perhaps it is just that one fool may easily recognise another. But it seems to me, even despite your total ignorance of the subject, that you are destined to play music, and just as surely that I am destined to teach you how. So take this instrument from me now and I will begin your first lesson." Then the man held out the strange object that was stranger than all the other strange objects, the morin khuur, for Thirsty Horse to take.

Now Thirsty Horse had listened very attentively to the man - yet he did not take the instrument. Instead, he just stood and looked at it, while he thought about what the man said; and then he thought about it some more – and then he burst into tears!

"What is it now!" asked the man, finally giving in to a feeling of exasperation that was rather more than simply justified.

"Oh, you are right, you are right." replied Thirsty Horse. "For now that I have heard music and understood what it is, there is no dearer wish in my heart than to play music myself. Yet I cannot, for I am a horse and I do not have hands and fingers like you." Then faced with this hopelessness Thirsty Horse just stood there, still and forlorn, looking imploringly at the man through his tears.

But the man only smiled and said, "Before we begin your first lesson in music, horse, here is your first lesson in life. Always look carefully at what is there, and see what is before your eyes. Now look carefully at your hands and learn this lesson well."

Then Thirsty Horse looked rather shyly down at where he expected the hooves of his fore legs to be - and saw to his tremendous surprise and delight that he had the arms and hands and fingers of a man! Although this should not have surprised him really, of course, for as he knew very well the Cup of Curiosity had made of him a boy, which is a foal of men; and a foal of men does not have hooves like a horse.

Once Thirsty Horse had fully grasped the reality of his situation, the man said, "Now horse, if I am to be your teacher then we must know of each other our names. So I introduce myself to you, and my name is Ertenbaatar. Please tell me your name?"

"Very pleased to meet you, Ertenbaatar." replied Thirsty Horse politely, "and my name – is Thirsty Horse."

Now it must be said that Ertenbaatar did look a little surprised when he heard this name. But after a few seconds thought it seemed to him to be a very good name for this horse that was now a boy. So he politely replied in his turn, "Yours is quite a strange name for a boy, Thirsty Horse. Yet it does seem to be a good name for you – for it tells of where you came. Nevertheless, I think that I will just call you Horse for short, if you don't mind."

"No. Not at all." said Thirsty Horse. "I don't mind at all." Although the thought did cross his mind that if 'Thirsty Horse' sounded like a strange name to Ertenbaatar – well, let's just say the sentiment worked just as well in reverse. But of course, Thirsty Horse was too polite to say.

"Very well then Horse." said Ertenbaatar. "Shall we begin your first lesson in music?"

"Yes." said Thirsty Horse with enthusiasm. "I would like that very much."

So they began the first lesson, and Ertenbaatar was pleased to note that he had been right to think, as indeed he had thought from the first moment that Thirsty Horse had listened to him play the morin khuur, that Thirsty Horse would be a very good pupil indeed.

...

Eventually Thirsty Horse stayed with Ertenbaatar for a whole year while he learned how to play the Morin Khuur – and of course he learned to sing too. In fact, Ertenbaatar taught him everything that he knew, and Thirsty Horse learned attentively and gratefully to all that he was taught.

There were some things that stayed in his mind more sharply than others, though; and here is one lesson that he remembered perhaps most of all:

"Tell me again," asked Thirsty Horse, "where should I stop the string to finish the music?"

Then he waited for the answer, but Ertenbaatar did not tell him. Instead, he looked Thirsty Horse straight in the eye and said, "Now, Horse, let us be clear on what it is that you wish to learn here. For certainly I can tell you where to stop the string. Yet there is only one place that is correct and your own ears can tell you where that is without any help from me. So tell me Horse, do you wish simply to repeat upon the strings the patterns that I tell you? Or do you wish to understand the music for yourself?

Then Thirsty Horse replied immediately and without any hesitation at all, "Teacher, I want to understand the music for myself." And a big smile came to his long horsey face as he said this, for his heart told him that his answer was right just as surely as his ear could tell him where to stop the string to sound the right note.

"You have chosen well, Horse." confirmed Ertenbaatar. "You have chosen well."

...

It was a sad day for both of them when finally the end of that year arrived and Ertenbaatar said, "I think, Horse, that now it is time for you to leave. You are a good musician, and although there is more that I could teach you, it is not much and your life beckons you to other things. What's more, you play well enough now that you will be able to earn a living from your music as you go."

Of course Thirsty Horse immediately burst into tears again when he heard this, because he loved Ertenbaatar and he had loved this time and the learning of music from his friend and first teacher. Yet in his heart he knew that this advice was wise and correct and so he did not try to argue that he stay. All he said was, "Yes, you are right, teacher. It is time for me to continue my journey to the end of the steppe and find the world of men. Then he looked Ertenbaatar squarely in the eye and said, "Although apart from this general idea, I do not know at all what I shall do."

Now Ertenbaatar smiled once more when he heard this, and using his pupil's full name for once replied, "Thirsty Horse, the next thing that you must do is to go to the big town on the edge of the steppe, and there you must go to school."

...

Chapter 4:
School

Thirsty Horse walked for several days before he reached the town on the edge of the steppe where the school was to be found, and on the way he passed several small settlements of men, which he now knew to be called "ger camps," because as well as music, Thirsty Horse had learnt the names of many things from Ertenbaatar.

Three times Thirsty Horse passed through one of these ger camps and each time he stopped there the night and played the morin khuur so that the people would be entertained. Then someone would always be happy to give him shelter for the night, and someone would always give him food. For the people of the steppe were friendly and kind, and as with most people who have very little, they were generous with the little they had.

Since he found no one to travel with him Thirsty Horse journeyed alone, just as he had when first he had left the herd. Since he was no longer a horse, however, he could not gallop as he had before but travelled at the speed of men, which seemed to him to be rather slow. Although he was pleased with the strength and endurance of his body all the same, because in making him a boy the Cup of Curiosity had respected his character as well as his origins as a horse, and Thirsty Horse was a very strong boy indeed.

Between the ger camps, Thirsty Horse spent his nights upon the open steppe – and yes, he listened to the wolves howl. Yet since he was now a boy he did not run from the wolves. Instead he lit a fire from wood that he carried with him, or sometimes found along the way, and then the wolves did not come close but stayed in the far distance, howling as they would. For just as the horses, the wolves were wary of men.

The Thirsty Horse of Mongolia

Now here was Thirsty Horse all alone upon the open steppe with nothing but the strength of his boy's body to protect himself with, and that was far from the strength that he had possessed as a horse. Yet the wolves were afraid of him now while they had not been before, and that seemed rather strange. In fact so strange did it seem to Thirsty Horse that he thought about this very carefully each night while he camped beneath the stars upon the open steppe beside the crackle and glow of his wood fire - and that is how he came to know the gifts of the stars to men. Once he knew these gifts he counted them out to himself each night before he slept, and these are the gifts as he counted them,

> "Imagination to be inspired; ingenuity to achieve and enough strength to achieve it with; courage to dare; intelligence to bind it all into one; memory to build upon, and compassion for all the world."

The last night that Thirsty Horse camped out upon the open steppe before he reached the town with the school, he came across quite a big ger camp and he stayed the night there. In the camp he played his music well, and as the people were lucky at that time with their provisions, so too were they generous in their appreciation and left him well stocked indeed when he left. So much so, in fact, that he almost regretted their generosity. For he was bowed quite low under the weight of all their gifts while he carried them in his sack upon his back.

...

When Thirsty Horse was close enough to the town with the school that he could see it upon the horizon he stopped - and he stared in wonder! For the sheer size of its construction came as such a shock to his imagination even while it remained as no more than a distant silhouette. When he came closer still he could make out that it was, in fact, a vast circle of gers surrounding enormous buildings with straight sides and angled corners. And these buildings, he saw, towered up to three, or four, or five times the height of a man - or even of a horse!

Enthralled by this new and wondrous vision, Thirsty Horse walked on ever closer, while his fascination lent speed to his step. Until finally he stood at the very frontier of the town, only a few steps from the first of its gers; and there he stopped to appreciate how big the town really was, now that he saw it so close.

It was not, he saw, like a ger camp that was spread out along a single track that passed through its centre. Instead, it was so grand that the sight of it appeared to march away from him to both left and right for as far as he could see. As for its streets, there must have been ten, or twenty, or even thirty streets perhaps. More, possibly, than anyone could ever count with certainty, let alone walk down them all and know where, each to the other, they were. While as for the number of people that it must take to live in such a huge place, surely that must be more than all the stars that glitter in the sky at night above the steppe, and that was many indeed. "But of course it has to be so," thought Thirsty Horse to himself, "for how many stars in the sky or people upon the earth must it take, before Man would build a school in which to teach his children?"

So big was the town that Thirsty Horse felt really quite nervous about crossing its border. But then he remembered the gifts of men that the steppe had taught him beneath its stars and that he counted out to himself each night. So Thirsty Horse set the gift of courage to shine within his heart before all others, and the gift of courage shone very brightly indeed. He sang too, as he walked, a song that Ertenbaatar had taught him: a song to the joy of life that told of hope and happiness - and that, of course, is a song that is sung in a major key.

...

Thirsty Horse quickly found the school by introducing himself politely to a solitary figure who happened to be passing by and then asking the way. The passer-by was actually quite startled by this rather wild and tough looking boy who had just wandered in to the town alone from the open steppe, and who called himself by such a strange name too. But he was pleased to help him nonetheless.

When Thirsty Horse arrived at the school it was late in the afternoon, but still early enough for the front door to be unlocked and for someone to be inside. So he went straight in and found, almost immediately, a rather important looking person.

"Hello." said the rather important looking person with just a little more than a hint of suspicion in his voice, "Can I help you?"

"Yes." said Thirsty Horse with the nonchalantly confident air of one who could play the morin khuur quite well. "I want to go to school."

"I'm sorry," said the important person, hardly even pausing to draw breath, "but you cannot. The session for this year will begin tomorrow and all the places are taken."

"Oh!" said Thirsty Horse; rather disappointed and now with the less than confident air of one who hadn't really thought through exactly how his ability to play the morin khuur quite well would get him into the school. Then Thirsty Horse stood quite still - and had no idea at all of what to do next. While the rather important looking person regarded him in a manner that no one would ever have called kind.

The silence lasted for just a few awkward moments more before the important looking person said curtly, "Next year." by way of a hint that Thirsty Horse was certainly not welcome now and would do better to come back then.

"But - but what will I do for a year?" cried Thirsty Horse as he suddenly found his voice again.

"Neither do I know, nor do I care." came the reply without sympathy. "But if I were you I would go now as quickly as possible. Because I am the Administrator for the affairs of the school - and if you do not, then I shall strike you off the register for next year as well."

Now for a moment Thirsty Horse was too shocked even to react at all. But then with sudden understanding and a terrible fear that this one year of delay really would become two, he let out a shriek and ran out of the school as fast as he could!

...

Once Thirsty Horse was outside again and safely distant from the threat of the School Administrator, he continued on walking slowly with his head down and his mind full of his problem of how to get into the school. Yet however much he thought, he could think of nothing that seemed of any use.

So deep was Thirsty Horse in his thoughts as he walked, that he did not notice a group of boys who lounged upon a rough bench by the side of the way where he passed. Not, that is, until one of the boys – the biggest and loudest and obviously the leader, called out to him, "Hey – you! Oo are you an' what are you doin' 'ere?"

Then Thirsty Horse looked up and saw the boys, and he thought to himself what friendly and kind boys they must be to be so concerned about him as to call out and ask these questions, just as he was walking by. With such trust in his heart as this inspired, and since at this moment he really needed some friendly help too, Thirsty Horse decided immediately to explain his woes to these boys and he replied honestly, "Oh! Thank you for your concern and perhaps you can help me. I must go to school, yet the school starts tomorrow and I have no place. But I cannot waste a year in waiting for I have drunk from the Cup of Curiosity and my mind will simply not stand to be still for so long. So please help me if you can, kind boys, and I will be so very grateful to you if you do."

Then the boys, seeing that this stranger was simple and sincere, decided that they would have some fun with him. While since they were actually not kind, nor even very nice boys at all, some profit from him too. So the leader of the boys said, in his very friendly, but strangely accented, voice, "Ah! You are so lucky to 'ave found us, stranger, for it would be our great pleasure to 'elp you an' surely we can guarantee that you will enter the school tomorrow. 'Cos we are all enrolled in the school and know very well, therefore, wot you must do."

"Oh! Wonderful, wonderful." replied Thirsty Horse excitedly, and he believed that now his luck had turned.

"But first." continued the leader of the boys. If we are to 'elp you – then surely you must pay for our 'elp. So 'ow much money 'ave you got?"

"Money?" replied Thirsty Horse. "But I have no money at all."

"Wot - nuffing? " replied the boy in surprise. But he regained his composure before he continued, "But – 'ow can that be! For if you 'ave no money at all, then 'ow do you pay for your way and the food wot you eat."

"I eat the food that people give me for the music that I play on my morin khuur" replied Thirsty Horse simply. "And although it is also true that sometimes people give me money in place of food, still it is never very much and at this time I have none."

Then the leader of the boys looked angry for a moment, although Thirsty Horse did not understand why, and said, "If you 'ave no money, stranger, then you must give us your morin."

"Oh! But that I cannot do." replied Thirsty Horse immediately. "For if I give you my morin khuur, then no one will give me any food to eat and surely I will starve to death! And what good would it do for me to go to school then?"

Now when he heard these words the leader of the boys realised that the stranger was not so stupid after all, and he wondered for a moment if there really was any profit to be had from this encounter. So he said, "If you 'ave nothing at all to give us, stranger, then we cannot 'elp you - and you cannot go to school!" And with that he turned his face dissmissively away.

"Wait!" cried Thirsty Horse as an idea suddenly came to him. "I am sorry that I do not have any money to offer you. But I am lucky today for I do have food indeed and all of that I will happily give you if only you will help me to go to school."

Now when the leader of the boys heard this proposition he thought about it for a moment, and then he asked, "Alright then, wot 'ave you got?"

"Many good things." replied Thirsty Horse. "Indeed in my sack, that you see here, I have bread and vegetables and fruits and sweets and all are good to eat; as well as milk and some wonderful fresh water to drink." Then Thirsty Horse opened his sack and took out all the wonderful things that he was offering to the boys.

Well the boys looked at Thirsty Horse's food for a few moments, and then they looked at each other, and then the leader said, "Okay stranger. We accept your offer."

Then before Thirsty Horse could say another word the boys fell like vultures upon all that he offered and very quickly ate and drank the lot. In fact not a single crumb nor drop did they leave for Thirsty Horse himself and not another word did they speak to him either until they had finished it all. As for Thirsty Horse, he waited patiently until there was nothing left. Then he looked expectantly at the leader of the boys and said, wondering too what he would now eat himself, "I am glad that you enjoyed all of my food so much. But now, kind boy, what about the school?"

"Ah! Yes!" said the leader of the boys, and a look came into his eyes as if he had just remembered their agreement. "Yes indeed. Now I will tell you wot to do an' give you wot you need to get into the school, even though you 'ave no money and pay us so little for the service. But fair is fair an' we must respect our deal."

Then the leader of the boys drew from his pocket a small box and said to Thirsty Horse, "The reason why you cannot get into the school, stranger, is quite simple. An' in fact you would know it yourself if you were not such a country person with no knowledge of our ways in the town." Then the boy showed the box to Thirsty Horse and said, "'ere is a packet that contains twenty sticks, which are called 'Sticks of Intelligence.' Wot you must do is to put each one in turn into your mouth, then light it with a match, an' suck in the smoke. Now watch and I will show you 'ow."

Then the boy took one of the Sticks of Intelligence from the packet and put it in his mouth. He lit in with a match, and then he leaned back and proceeded to smoke it slowly, with a look of deep satisfaction on his face.

"You see, stranger?" said the boy. "You see 'ow intelligent an' sophisticated I am now? Anyone can see this, just as you; and that, of course, is why they let me into the school."

"Yes, yes! I see!" said Thirsty Horse excitedly. For he could indeed see how intelligent and sophisticated the leader of the boys now appeared to be as he smoked the Stick of Intelligence.

"Good." said the boy. "Now, I 'ave taken one so there are nineteen of these Sticks of Intelligence left in this packet. You should smoke all of 'em now to make up for your lost time. Then when people see you tomorrow they will know immediately that you are wise an' knowledgeable like us boys - an' of course, the school will be very pleased to let you in for this year." Then the leader of the boys handed the Sticks of Intelligence, together with the matches, to Thirsty Horse.

"Thank you, thank you – ever so much." said Thirsty Horse and he eagerly took the packet. Then with just a little help from the leader of the boys to learn the technique of smoking, Thirsty Horse began to smoke very quickly all the Sticks in the packet.

Now it was a very strange thing, since Thirsty Horse knew that the Sticks would make him more intelligent, but as he smoked he began to feel ill! Still he continued with the smoking, thinking that the feeling would pass. But strangely it did not - and even got worse, which he could not understand at all.

Of course he courageously continued with the smoking, since his education depended upon it, and he fought against the terrible burning in his lungs and the awful coughing that came to him. But by the time that he had nearly finished all of the Sticks of Intelligence in the packet, his head had begun to spin too and he was beginning to feel really dizzy! Bravely he took one puff more, but then he became so very dizzy that he could not even stand up; and finally he simply fell to the ground and lay moaning and groaning in the dust.

So Thirsty Horse lay pained and writhing in this terrible condition and perhaps even dying for all he knew. Yet he hardly even cared, for his head was aching so badly that he could not think about anything else at all - not even the school. There was one other thing that he was aware of, though, for he did not have to think at all to know it - and that was the sound of the "kind boys" laughing loudly to themselves at the sight of him in this condition.

Now it seemed very strange to Thirsty Horse that these boys should find his terrible condition to be so funny. But there was worse yet to come – much worse! For once the boys began to grow tired of laughing at him he heard the leader say, "Look 'ow clever we are, us boys. For 'ere is a country fool wot we 'ave tricked - an' now we can take everyfing wot 'e 'as." Then the leader of the boys grabbed hold of Thirsty Horse's beloved morin khuur, while another boy took his sack, and yet another took his boots from his feet. Then they all laughed all the more loudly once again.

Thirsty Horse, however, although he was very much down, was not beaten yet. For he had one last trick to play, as the Cup of Curiosity had wisely provided that he should. So Thirsty Horse fought down the pains that ricocheted now around and around within his head, and he murmured aloud as best he could the magic words, "Boy, be a horse again!"

Suddenly the air was split by the sound of a huge clap of thunder and before the boys there stood a horse, although a rather unsteady horse it must be said. Yet if Thirsty Horse could no longer stand upon two legs as a boy, he didn't find it quite so hard to stand upon four legs as a horse. Then as the boys stopped their laughing and stared open mouthed at this miraculous and unexpected transformation, Thirsty Horse began to rear and buck and with all his hooves to aim kicks at them as best he could. Now in the condition that he was in it is no surprise that Thirsty Horse did not hit a single boy with a single kick, and of course that was fortunate since it can be a serious matter to be kicked by a horse. The sight of him trying to, though, was quite enough to make the "kind boys" drop everything that they had taken and run in fear of their lives, and that was good fortune indeed.

Once they had gone, Thirsty Horse groaned to himself with little enthusiasm, "Horse, be a boy again." and as soon as the transformation was complete he gathered all his belongings together once more and crawled pathetically underneath the bench that the boys had been sitting on. Then clutching all his possessions to him so that no one could attempt to steal them again without disturbing him, he escaped from the torments of his body by falling gratefully asleep.

...

When Thirsty Horse woke up it was very early in the morning and he was still underneath the bench. While on the bench, and completely unaware of Thirsty Horse, a man was sitting quietly.

Since Thirsty Horse was awake now - he moved, and as he moved he felt a pain once more in his head. So he groaned with the pain, "Oh! Oh!" and startled the man, who then saw him.

Now this man, who was in fact very respectable and rather well dressed, was at first quite shocked by the sight of Thirsty Horse in

such a state as he was and indeed he thought him to be a tramp or such low person. But then the man noticed that Thirsty Horse was just a boy and he wondered what the truth might really be. For here, by chance, was a man of whom it was said that he would never leave a child in trouble if ever he knew there was. Since he was, too, a courageous man and had no more fear, should he be wrong, of a tramp than of a boy, he asked Thirsty Horse who he was and what had happened to leave him in such a state.

In order to answer respectfully the man's questions, and not simply to speak from the ground, Thirsty Horse stood up - and then what a terrible state he showed himself to be in, for he had been ever so sick before he slept and all his clothes as well as his face were covered in his own vomit. Yet once he stood up he felt steady again on his feet; his headache was just a dull pain now, and in his stomach he felt no more than a ravenous hunger. What's more, he was still the same innocent and trusting soul that he had always been. So since the man asked, and since Thirsty Horse trusted him on sight, he told the man the story of the kind boys, of the Sticks of Intelligence, of being ill, and of spending the night under the bench; although the other details of the story he didn't tell. When he had finished his story he said, in a voice that was nothing less than the pure spirit of innocence betrayed, "Oh what a fool I have been to have so trusted those boys."

Now when the man heard these last words of Thirsty Horse offered in sincere and serious culmination to his story, he rolled back his head and laughed very, very loudly indeed. Louder, even, than the "kind boys" had laughed, which made Thirsty Horse think to himself that his life could never be worse than this. For here he had trusted once again, and yet the man was crueller still than the boys. All the while that the man laughed, Thirsty Horse sat in misery upon the bench beside him, although not too close of course, and he considered unhappily how cruel life was.

Life, however, was not so cruel, at least on that day, as Thirsty Horse had believed it to be. For when the man finally stopped laughing he looked very kindly at Thirsty Horse; and then he said, "It is indeed an interesting tale that you tell, Thirsty Horse, although rather unfortunate for yourself - and certainly I would call you foolish with your trust. Yet foolishness by goodness of heart does not quite make a fool, while for your sincerity and your honesty, and for the suffering that your search for an education has brought to you, for that you have earned my respect. But what I envy you for, Thirsty Horse, is your luck. Because I, whom you have so amused and impressed with your tale of woe, I am the teacher of the school, and I offer you now a place for this year starting from when we both arrive at the gate. Although," continued the teacher, "that will not be for a few minutes yet - because no boy who attends my school is ever going to pass its gate in such a disgusting state as you are now, Thirsty Horse. So on our way to the school we will pass by the river and you will jump in and wash yourself for as long as it takes to get clean again!"

...

That is the story of how Thirsty Horse got into the school. As for the kind boys, though, he did not find them there, for they had lied to him and did not go to school. In fact he never saw them again for as long as he lived. And of course, neither did he ever smoke one of the Sticks of Intelligence again either.

...

Chapter 5:
The Town on the Edge
of the Steppe

On the morning of the first day that Thirsty Horse went to school the teacher said, "Class. If you are to order your lives to make the best use of your time here, then you must have a routine."

"A routine!" thought Thirsty Horse to himself, and he wondered what that might be. He very quickly found out, of course, and then he thought it to be a rather strange idea indeed! But then you must remember that until quite recently Thirsty Horse had been a horse who lived free upon the open steppe, and this formative experience did tend to colour his thinking from time to time. Nevertheless he soon fell into the pattern of his routine, which was invariably the same each day for five days of every week from Monday to Friday - for indeed that is what a routine is.

The routine began with Thirsty Horse sneaking carefully past the School Administrator, who would scowl at him menacingly if he saw him. Then for several minutes, or longer if he came early to avoid the scowl, Thirsty Horse would stand quietly outside the classroom with the other pupils. At 8:30 a.m. exactly the teacher would arrive; he would open the door and go inside, and the class would solemnly follow him in.

Now at first Thirsty Horse found this "routine" idea to be a very strange way to live - but he coped with it. While the next thought that he had about the "routine" came after about two weeks and was much harder to keep under control. For one morning, when Thirsty Horse had just finished successfully sneaking past the School Administrator, he found that he wanted to laugh at the whole idea, which suddenly seemed quite ridiculous to him! Indeed so ridiculous did the "routine" seem to him that day, that he found it difficult even to remain properly solemn in the classroom. Fortunately the humour passed, though; and it was fortunate too that he managed to cope with the situation before it did, since it is very unlikely that the teacher would have appreciated the humour of the situation quite as much as his pupil.

Eventually Thirsty Horse did get used to his school routine and he concluded that it was not such a bad thing after all. For it was a simple procedure that began the day on a note of respect and helped him to order his thoughts. With this understanding finally in its proper place he breathed a contented sigh of relief and moved on to other, more interesting, things: such as the magic of deciphering the mysterious squiggles of writing into words; of learning the geography of the world - or a new song to sing and to play on the morin khuur.

As for his lessons in the school, Thirsty Horse found these to be fascinating and mostly difficult to understand. While the teacher noted that Thirsty Horse always looked very hard to find what there was of interest in any subject, and concluded that that was why he generally found it.

As for why he found his lessons to be difficult, you must remember once again that Thirsty Horse had been a horse until very recently and that that was the basis of his character. For upon that basis he was a big strong boy who worked very hard, but he was not so very clever. On the other hand, though, he had a most wonderful imagination that had grown from always looking to the horizon over a vast land - and so it may be said too, if you think about it, that the Cup of Curiosity had chosen his disciple well.

Indeed, true to his character, Thirsty Horse always did his best. So although he started off well below even the bottom of the class, he managed, after a while, to bring his marks up to at least a respectable level. Sometimes, though, he would get very good marks indeed, although he really had no idea why. Not, that is, until one day when the teacher took pity on him in his bewilderment and explained it to him like this, "Thirsty Horse. Before you came to school you lived upon the open steppe and not in the town, and so everything is new and different to you here and often you find that your lessons are difficult and hard to understand. Yet from time to time, even so, we find ourselves studying something that you can understand more easily than anyone else in the class simply because you do see things differently from us. Since, too, you have a talent to communicate what you understand, it is then that I give you the best marks of all."

Of course, Thirsty Horse was very happy when the teacher praised him like this, and he was not at all modest in accepting this rare accolade. Perhaps he was a little disgruntled, therefore, that before he could really enjoy it the teacher added this post script to his praise. "Now it is all very well to get the top mark of the class once every now and again, Thirsty Horse. But it is not that which really impresses me." at which Thirsty Horse's disappointment began to show on his face. Not for very long though, as the teacher continued, "It is the simple fact that you always try so hard that really impresses me, Thirsty Horse. For I see that by your efforts to tell us what you know, you have made of your ability to communicate a talent far greater than your gift."

So that was how it went at school and Thirsty Horse enjoyed learning on every day that passed. In fact the only black note that he could think of was having to sneak past the scowl of the School Administrator every morning before his lessons began.

. . .

Now Thirsty Horse, just like most people, had two halves of his life to organise. So to return once again to that first day when he had got into the school, it was on the evening of that very same day that he had found the other half of his life waiting for him once school had finished. For then he had to find something to eat and somewhere to live, and how to provide for that living.

As for somewhere to live, he carefully selected a ger that he liked the look of and knocked on the door. Then as soon as the door opened he introduced himself as Thirsty Horse, explained that he played the morin khuur to pay his way, and stated that he was looking for a place to stay. Then he announced most proudly of all that he was a pupil in the school and he finished with a smile, fully expecting to be offered the hospitality of the occupants. Yet in this, Thirsty Horse had miscalculated. For here was the town and not the open steppe, and people who lived in the town did not say to themselves, "If not I then who?" So the answer came back, "Good luck, Thirsty Horse, but we have no place for you here." - and Thirsty Horse found himself still standing in the cold night air while the door of the ger before him remained firmly closed.

"Oh!" he said to himself. For in fact he was rather surprised.

Since there was nothing else that Thirsty Horse could do except continue, however, that is exactly what he did. He passed ger after ger and repeated the same words, only to get the same result. While the explanation that he gave in the same way each time became a routine, which was the second time on that day that Thirsty Horse had come across the idea.

Eventually, however, he did find a ger where the occupant did not wish him simply good luck and good bye. Instead, the man regarded him rather suspiciously and said, "Hmm? If you play the morin khuur to earn your living, as you say. Then by the look of you I would say that you do not play it very well." which statement, under the circumstances, appeared to Thirsty Horse as rather more of a chance than a condemnation, and therefore caused him no offence at all.

Quickly he took his morin khuur from his back and without saying another word he began to play and to sing a slow and languorous rhapsody of longing for the open steppe. He played this music because the thought had occurred to him that since the man in the ger lived in the town he would know this sentiment in his heart – and of course he was right. As soon as the man heard the music play he shed a tear from his eye and immediately invited Thirsty Horse to come and stay with him forever, which was actually quite a lot longer than Thirsty Horse had in mind. Due to the difficulty of finding accommodation, however, he decided not to say anything about that for now and gratefully accepted the offer.

As for food? Well actually, the teacher had given him some food when the school had broken for lunch that day. True it wasn't much and Thirsty Horse had eaten all of it within minutes of receiving it, but at least he did not go completely hungry.

So that took care of Thirsty Horse's problem of accommodation, and his immediate hunger. Yet he still had to earn enough to pay his way; and of course he really did have nothing more to eat. So once he had suitably thanked the man in the ger he left his sack behind and wondered off into the town in search of a suitable spot to sing and to play for his supper.

...

After a few weeks of living in the town, Thirsty Horse became very well known for his singing and playing - and quite appreciated too. While since he had also come to terms with the idea of a "routine" at school, it occurred to him that perhaps he should introduce a routine into his playing as well, and so that is what he did. For three evenings at the end of each week, Thirsty Horse would hold a concert and play music for any who came. Then for the rest of the week he mostly studied by himself in the ger or practised his playing of the morin khuur, which all in all he found to be a satisfactory way to organise his life. He did not charge anything for the concerts that he gave, but only asked that people should give him some food or some small thing, if they had it. Just enough, in fact, that he could eat and have something left to give each week to the man in the ger and his family, to repay a little more their hospitality.

Now when he was not at school, nor studying at home or practising the morin khuur, nor playing in his concerts, and not sleeping, Thirsty Horse would often wander through the streets of the town to see what he could find, which is how he came to be talking, one evening, to a man who advised him, "You know, Thirsty Horse, it is not fair that you ask nothing for what you do. For you work hard to play music and you are very talented. People take from you something of value, and although they are mostly of good heart, still many of them give you nothing in return."

Thirsty Horse thought about this for a moment, and then he replied, "I do not ask because I give what I have from my heart and my greatest pleasure is to give. While what I receive, in fact, is enough."

Yet the man replied, "All that you say is good, Thirsty Horse. But still people rarely value what is given free, no matter how much it is really worth."

"Hmm?" said Thirsty Horse, and he thought about this some more.

While the man, seeing that Thirsty Horse was still not convinced, continued, "I'll tell you what, Thirsty Horse, I will offer you now my advice, and you may accept it or ignore it as you wish. But it is well meant." Then the man explained, "Each week when you hold your first concert, hold it for free and invite all the poorest people from the town. Then play for yourself and for your own pleasure. Play just simple happy songs from your heart and let the people sing with you too if they will. At your second concert of the week play music that is serious, and at your last concert of the week play music that is new, or that is more difficult again. For each of these two later concerts, ask for a set entrance fee - although it need not be much and it can be money or food as people wish.

"If you do this, then you will be playing different music each time. You will attract people with different musical appreciation to each concert, and I think you will find that more people will come. From more people you will take more by way of entrance fee, and so from what you take at these concerts you should keep for yourself a fair wage, which is right and just because you will have earned it. If you find that you have more than you need, then the difference will be yours to use as you will and you can distribute it to the poor if you wish. But whether you do or not, I think that if you follow this suggestion then everybody will be better off one way or another; and I am sure too, at least for myself, that all will respect you more for your music than they did before."

Now the more that Thirsty Horse thought about this suggestion, the more it seemed to him like a good idea. So finally that is what he did, and he was very pleased to find that the results were just as the man had said they would be. The early concert of each week was popular with everyone, and Thirsty Horse saw that just as many of the better off came on this evening and enjoyed to sing together. While as for the later two concerts of the week, they were better attended than ever before too, and so the idea did indeed work well for all.

Thirsty Horse continued to run this program of concerts in exactly this manner for quite a few weeks. But then since he had now been made aware of the possibilities for diversity and organisation, he decided to think about the situation a bit more and see if he couldn't do even better still. Then after a little thought he decided to make the second concert a recital of classical musical poems, which he loved but which took quite some patience to understand and to appreciate. While at the last concert of the week he would open with a short classical piece of particular note and then present a selection of his own compositions, for he did indeed compose a little himself too. To finish in fine mood he would conclude with some very happy songs; and just as he had hoped it would this combination worked even better still, which rather suggested to Thirsty Horse that there were, perhaps, even more and better possibilities yet. But then again, he was quite successful enough for now and so he decided to leave such exploration until later, which I think was a very wise choice.

...

So Thirsty Horse was at school, he lived comfortably with the family in the Ger, he ate well enough and he enjoyed his concerts; and in fact his life was as much in harmony as a well rehearsed musical composition. Except, that is, for the single wrong note that still sounded to mar this harmony - and that, of course, was the same single wrong note that had been there since the first day he had begun school. For each morning Thirsty Horse was still obliged to sneak carefully past the School Administrator to avoid his scowl.

Now one Sunday afternoon Thirsty Horse was wandering around the town, looking here and there to see if there would be some new thing of interest to discover, and thinking all the time about this particular problem. He was just thinking too that it was a shame that he could not find anything new to distract him from it, when he came across a man dressed in such a strange fashion that Thirsty Horse could not stop himself from staring in fascination. What the man was wearing was a long, plain robe but of a very bright colour; and that was unusual enough to make Thirsty Horse think that here, surely, was

someone who would distract him from his problem, which did indeed prove to be the case. For as soon as the strangely dressed man saw Thirsty Horse looking at him, he called out to him in a friendly voice, although with words that were certainly inspired by the rudeness of Thirsty Horse's staring, "Hello, boy with the long face like a horse." Then he asked politely, "How are you today?"

"Very well, thank you." replied Thirsty Horse just as politely, "and how are you?"

"Very well." replied the man.

"Then may I ask," Thirsty Horse continued, "why you are dressed so strangely?"

"You may ask," replied the man, "and I will tell you." Then by way of explanation he continued, " I am dressed like this to show that I have dedicated my life to understanding and have no need of worldly things."

"That is very interesting!" exclaimed Thirsty Horse. "But what exactly does it mean?"

Now at this question the man paused for a moment or two, and then he did not answer the question but rather replied inquisitively, "What is your name, boy with a long face like a horse?" and Thirsty Horse told him his name.

"Well that is an unusual name," said the man in the strange clothes. "Yet I must admit that it seems to me, even after so short a time, that it is a good name for you. For you do indeed have a long face like a horse, and I would say a little of the character of one too."

"Thank you." said Thirsty Horse, and he took an innocent pride in these compliments, for compliments they most certainly were as far as he was concerned.

"Well then, Thirsty Horse." continued the man. "Let me try and answer your question like this." Then he asked, "Do you not wonder why the world has come to be, and are you not grateful for your life?"

Now Thirsty Horse was quite surprised by this question, but without any hesitation at all he replied, " As for why the world has come to be, that I do not know. But as for my life, for that I am certainly grateful."

At which the man smiled and said, "Indeed it is true, Thirsty Horse, that you have the character of a horse. For with your eyes you see exactly what is before you but no more, while in your heart you see clearly what is good and what is bad. But please answer me one question," continued the man," and then he asked,

"Just before you go to sleep each night, Thirsty Horse. Do you not say some words of gratitude that the world is so, even if you do not understand why?"

Now this was a very strange question indeed and Thirsty Horse was not sure at first that he understood it at all. In fact he thought about it for quite several seconds before he could think of a reply. But then suddenly an idea came to him and he knew with certainty exactly what answer he should give,

"Yes!" he replied. "Yes. Of course I do."

At which it was the man in the long, colourful robe who looked surprised. "Then what do you say?" he asked with interest and more than a little suspicion.

"Every night before I sleep," said Thirsty Horse, "I simply count to myself the gifts to men, which I understood beneath the stars when I camped upon the open steppe." Then Thirsty Horse recited the gifts: "Imagination to be inspired; ingenuity to achieve and enough strength to achieve it with; courage to dare; intelligence to bind it all into one; memory to build upon, and compassion for all the world."

Now when the man heard these words he lost his look of suspicion completely and in its place put a smile of great satisfaction. "Ah!" he said. "Then you really do know gratitude for your life, Thirsty Horse. But tell me - surely there was someone who taught you these words?"

"No." replied Thirsty Horse. "There was no one. But then no one had need to either. For this is something that came to me very clearly one night while I camped upon the open steppe beneath the stars and wondered why the wolves did not dare to eat me."

Then the man's face took on a very solemn expression and he said, "Thirsty Horse, now I understand that you do indeed have a gift to see and to understand what you see, and that gift is far greater than I had thought. That gift is your destiny and it leads you to your future, although as yet you know it not yourself. But I know, and I will say no more to you now but rather leave your gift to teach you as it will. While all that I would wish for myself is this: that we may meet again when you have travelled a little further along the path of your life, and then that we may talk once more." And there the man in the strangely colourful robe fell still and silent, and for just a little while did nothing except to solemnly regard the long horsey face of the boy.

"But before we part, Thirsty Horse," the man recommenced when he was ready, "tell me if there is any way in which I may help you? Since that indeed would be my pleasure."

"Oh! Thank you indeed, kind man in the long and colourful robe." said Thirsty Horse. "I am very happy to hear your offer and it is most certainly appreciated. As for how you may help me, though, I do not think that you can. For I have only one problem in my life and I do not think that you will be able to help me with that."

"Perhaps not," said the man, "but tell me first your problem, Thirsty Horse, and then we will see."

So Thirsty Horse explained to the man in the long colourful robe all about the one wrong note that continued to mar the harmony of his life: the School Administrator and of having to sneak past him every morning to avoid his scowl. Thirsty Horse told the story from the very beginning, while the man in the long colourful robe listened very carefully to every word.

Once Thirsty Horse had finished telling the story, however, the man smiled at Thirsty Horse a smile of simple amusement. Then he took from somewhere inside his robe a small wooden carving of a figure that was really quite beautiful and he gave it to Thirsty Horse.

"Take this figure with my blessing," said the man, "and give it to the School Administrator the very next time that you see him. Say that you got it from a man dressed as I and that you wish him happiness and prosperity for all his life – and that will solve your problem."

Now Thirsty Horse was a little bit surprised when he heard this. But without any further questions he said trustingly. "Thank you, man in the long and colourful robe, and I will do that."

So the very next day when Thirsty Horse went to school he did exactly as the man in the long colourful robe had said - and the School Administrator looked very surprised indeed. But from that day on he was always very pleased to see Thirsty Horse and he replaced his scowl with a smile, for which Thirsty Horse was very grateful.

Now Thirsty Horse, at the time, couldn't understood what it was that had brought about this change; since from himself, the school administrator, and all of the reality of the situation, nothing was really any different than it had been before. It was quite sometime later when the thought occurred to him that even though nothing had changed in reality, it was, perhaps, in other terms that the change that taken place: in terms of the perception of one person of another, perhaps? "Yes." thought Thirsty Horse to himself then with sudden understanding. "The prejudice of that first meeting was removed that day – and that was the miracle of the gift from the man in the strangely coloured robe."

...

Chapter 6:
Last Day at School, and
What have you Learned?

In August the steppe is at its warmest and it is pleasant to travel and to sleep out under the stars; which was obviously why, Thirsty Horse though to himself, the school year lasted from the first of September to the end of July. It was May when this thought crossed his mind, and although there was still snow upon the ground, the wind carried with it the promise of warmth soon to come. All in all it was enough to make him think of summer and of travel, and to realise that his time at school was drawing to a close.

It was also by May that Thirsty Horse had completed enough of his studies for him to think that there was not much left of the world of men that he did not already know, and that all that remained for him to do was to see it for himself. That just as with the morin khuur, in fact, whose strings he knew now from the highest note to the lowest and all the art of musicianship that lay between, so too this moment approached with his education. In fact Thirsty Horse was beginning to think that he pretty well knew it all and had even become quite at risk of looking down his rather long nose at those who didn't.

So it was just, to say the least, that this thorn of arrogance sprouting to mar the gentle simplicity of his character should meet with a timely end. But it was not at school that Thirsty Horse would learn the error of his assumption. For it was music, strangely enough, that taught him this lesson.

Now there was one particular Ger in the town that Thirsty Horse would visit quite frequently, for it was the Ger of a man who made and sold musical instruments: drums and whistles and morin khuurs, of course; and also strings for the morin khuurs, which require to be renewed from time to time. Since Thirsty Horse visited this Ger quite frequently, and since he and the man would sometimes play music together too, he knew the man very well. Due to all of this creative activity by the man, what's more, Thirsty Horse usually referred to the man simply as 'Music Maker,' which the man did not contradict since he was rather pleased by it, although it was not actually his name.

What Thirsty Horse didn't know, however, was that Music Maker sometimes made other musical instruments apart from drums and whistles and morin khuurs. In fact he did not even guess that it could be so, for of such things as these he had never even so much as heard tell.

So it was that on one particular occasion when Thirsty Horse visited Music Maker, he found inside his ger a musical instrument that not only had he never seen before, but that challenged the very limits of his imagination from the first moment he saw it. Actually it was not unlike a morin khuur, although it had a body of a rather different shape, but what was most incredible about it was that it had six strings instead of two! As to how those strings could be played, however, that really was a puzzle! For the strings were all arranged flat in relation to the body of the instrument and it seemed, therefore, impossible that the bow could ever single any one of them out! Save for the outermost two, of course. After considering this aspect thoughtfully for a minute or two, Thirsty Horse was forced to accept the obvious and to conclude that all six strings should be bowed at once. But what on earth, he wondered, would such a complicated harmony as that sound like?

Indeed what would it sound like? And so compelled was Thirsty Horse to find out that he immediately seized hold of the wondrous instrument, grabbed a bow from a morin khuur nearby, commenced to scratch away at its strings - and to make the most horrible sound imaginable in the process! For this was not, of course, the correct way to play the instrument at all.

It was quite enough, however, to shock Music Maker out of his state of sly amusement. For he had been secretly watching Thirsty Horse with the new instrument and quite enjoying his young friend's naive reactions to it. He had not even so much as suspected that Thirsty Horse could be quite so innocent of it as he really was – but he certainly no longer doubted it now! In fact as soon as he heard the horrible noise, Music Maker realised that Thirsty Horse had absolutely no idea at all how to play the new instrument, and so he came rushing over to stop him before he did any damage.

"No! No!" he shouted. "Stop, Thirsty Horse! Stop before you break the bow!"

Then Thirsty Horse stopped his bowing and stared at Music Maker with such a look of puzzlement upon his face that now Music Maker could not help himself from bursting into laughter at the sight of him.

By the time he had stopped laughing, though, Music Maker was quite ready to explain all about the new instrument, and this he did. "Thirsty Horse," he began. "Please excuse my assumption, but I really thought that you would at least know what this instrument is, even if you have never seen one before. Since you obviously do not, however, I will introduce it to you. It is called a guitar, and it is not played with a bow."

"Really!" said Thirsty Horse, both fascinated and surprised by this revelation. "Then how is it played?"

"There are two ways." continued Music Maker. "You may play it with a pick, which is a small flat piece of tortoise shell. Or you may use another technique, which is called the classical technique, and play it with the nails of your fingers. Then Music Maker, who could play the guitar quite well, demonstrated both of these techniques to Thirsty Horse.

Now while Thirsty Horse watched Music Maker as he played the new instrument, he found himself to be really quite impressed. First of all by the technique of playing with the pick, and particularly by the way in which Music Maker could make all six strings sound in harmony at once, for this was just as he had imagined the instrument would be bowed. Yet when Music Maker showed him the classical technique, he was even more impressed still.

In fact so impressed was Thirsty Horse that he just had to try for himself. So once Music Maker had finished his demonstration, he took the guitar, and began immediately to practice the technique. Then he played - and he played - and he played; and indeed the hours passed quickly for him while he did.

The hours didn't pass quite so quickly for Music Maker, however, and after he had spent several of them assisting and listening to Thirsty Horse as he learnt to play the guitar he had reached the point where he had really heard enough. It was, in any case, nearly midnight by now; and since Thirsty Horse still gave no obvious sign that he was ever going to stop, Music Maker finally said in exasperation, "Thirsty Horse, take this guitar and go and practice playing it somewhere else. You can come back in a few days time and tell me whether you wish to buy it from me or not."

Now in truth this did seem to be a very fair suggestion to Thirsty Horse and he was fully intending to accept it as soon as he had reached a convenient point in his practising to stop. So it was somewhat of a shame, therefore, that before he had reached this convenient point Music Maker's patience came suddenly to a very abrupt end! Seizing the nearby morin khuur in both hands he wielded it high in the air as if he were about to smash it down on Thirsty

Horse's head; and he screamed, "Thirsty Horse, take the guitar and get out of my ger now!"; which certainly succeeded, finally, in getting his young friend's attention. So Thirsty Horse finally left the ger, and taking the guitar with him, went home – or rather ran in fear of his life from the wrath of Music Maker's temper, I should say.

Actually, Thirsty Horse found that it was not at all easy to learn how to play the guitar properly, and during the last months of the school year that remained to him, he came back many times to take lessons from Music Maker. These were lessons not only in guitar playing technique, what's more, but also in music itself. For the guitar was not at all the same instrument as the morin khuur, and with its six strings it required an understanding of music, and particularly of musical harmony, that Thirsty Horse had never even dreamt of while he sawed away with his bow at the two strings of the later instrument. But eventually Thirsty Horse did become just as good at playing the guitar as he had been at playing the morin khuur. Then since the instrument inspired him further by its greater possibilities he became better still, until eventually, he was really very good indeed.

So that is the story of how Thirsty Horse came to learn how to play the guitar. Yet what it had taught him most of all was that no matter how much he knew, he could never know how much was still left for him to learn; and he would never again assume that he did.

...

The last week at school was a time of happiness indeed for teacher and pupils alike. There was no more pressure to study hard since all the exams had been taken the week before and there was, too, a sense of accomplishment in everyone. All the pupils had passed their exams, although some better than others of course as is only natural with people anywhere. Yet there was one question that arose in the minds of some in the class to cast just a little doubt upon the moment. For there were some who wondered why, with the exams finished, they were still there at all?

"Because the last week at school," the teacher explained, "should serve us differently from the year past. We should use it to think about what we have learned and how we may best put those lessons to use. We should use it to recognise the pleasure that we have taken in the exercise of learning itself, as well as to be grateful for the benefit of the education that we have received. But what we should think about most of all," he continued, "is how best we may use our minds from now on.

"Truly the greatest part of the education that you have received at this school," he continued, "is not at all in the knowledge that you have learned, but rather it is in the training that you have received in the use of your mind. For it must be the goal of any good education to create a mind that is at once disciplined but at the same time free to build new ideas upon the structure of its knowledge. And that is the lesson that you should learn in this last week at school.

"So, pupils, you are free to ask any question that you would like and I will answer you if I can. Or at least, I hope, give you a respectable excuse if I cannot."

Now this was indeed a most noble sentiment and very well expressed too. Yet as many a teacher has often remarked it is not always easy to coax a pupil's mind to form a new question within the framework of his learning, however much it may be desired. So it was that during just such a moment as this, when the inspiration was not driving quite as it should in the intellects of his students, that the teacher decided to select a member of his class and give the situation a little prompt.

"Thirsty Horse." he picked his candidate. "I am very pleased with your work and I would like to know why it is that you always work so hard. Perhaps, indeed, the secret of your motivation may be of benefit to others in the class as well."

Now Thirsty Horse did not hesitate at all before he accepted to reply for the answer to this question was the very reason that had led him to drink from the Cup of Curiosity in the first place. What's more, he thought, that story would be such an interesting tale to tell his teacher, that he was anxious not to miss this chance that had finally arrived to do so. With a year's education now behind him, however, he would have done better to reconsider his story in that light before launching straight into it and simply telling all as he remembered it to be.

"Teacher," he began enthusiastically, "I learn because I am curious to know, and even though I do not need to really, because I only need to know the answer to one question - and that I have already."

"Really!" said the teacher, quite fascinated by this statement. "Then please, Thirsty Horse, tell us more of your story."

"Certainly." replied Thirsty Horse confidently; and this time, because by now he trusted everyone there, the told his whole story exactly as it was.

"It was at the end of August two years ago," he began, "and when I was still a horse. It was a beautiful summer's day and I should have been content just to graze by the river with the other horses. Yet I could not for there was an idea in my head that was tormenting me so and it would not leave me alone. My idea was to run all the way to the end of the steppe, even though I knew, as all the horses know, that the steppe never ends - but I had to prove it for myself.

"So I set out on my way, and I galloped and galloped and galloped until the sun was almost gone. By then I was very tired, of course, and I would have stopped to rest. But before I could I was chased by wolves and I had to run faster than I had ever run before to escape them; and then I had to run even more, for I knew that if I did not find the end of the steppe soon, then the wolves would still catch me and eat me anyway. So I ran until the sun had completely gone and it was really dark before finally I had to stop. But then I found myself in a village of men and so I knew that at last I was safe from the wolves.

"In that village I heard the sound of a river coming from inside one of the gers and so I entered it to drink. Once I was inside the ger, however, I did not find a river at all but only a cup full of water. Of course I was disappointed at not finding the river, but I was so very thirsty by then that I was grateful at least to drink from the cup. The cup, however, was a magic cup that could speak and it introduced itself to me as the 'Cup of Curiosity.' So I told my story to the Cup of Curiosity, and then the cup promised that it would make me a boy for five years, of which two have almost passed. During these five years I have to find out the answer to the question that the Cup asked me. Then if my answer is correct the Cup will make me a man."

"And if your answer is wrong?" asked the teacher, who was actually too amazed by the rest of the story to react to it in any other way - as indeed was everyone else in the class too.

"Then I must become a horse again." replied Thirsty Horse.

"Interesting." said the teacher, still completely stunned by this incredible recital. "And which, do you think, you would rather be?"

Then Thirsty Horse replied, and very respectfully too, "Teacher, I would rather be a man. For although I loved my life as a horse, and I loved to run upon the open steppe and to eat the fresh grass covered with the morning dew, really there was no more to it than that and my mind, even then, was not satisfied by that alone.

"Then tell us, Thirsty Horse." inquired the teacher. "Tell us your question and tell us your answer and then perhaps we will know whether you will become a man in three years time, or as yet risk to become a horse again."

"As for the question." answered Thirsty Horse. "The question is, "What is the secret of life?""

"Ah!" said the teacher, "Not such a simple question at all! And the answer?"

"The answer," said Thirsty Horse with an air of knowing pride, "Is that nothing is free."

Now for a few seconds after Thirsty Horse had spoken there was complete silence in the classroom. But then the teacher started to laugh, and after him everyone started to laugh – and they laughed and laughed and laughed! In fact they laughed so much that it made Thirsty Horse think again of the "kind boys" and the "sticks of intelligence," and indeed he became quite upset while he listened to their laughter.

When eventually they stopped laughing the teacher said. "I think, Thirsty Horse, that once again you have been just a little too quick to believe what others tell you. For what you have said, although it is an obvious truth in its way, cannot really be considered to be the secret of life."

Then Thirsty Horse thought about this for a moment, and as he thought about it he realised that what the teacher had said was true, which made him feel really rather foolish. Then as well as feeling rather foolish he began to feel rather dispirited, since he had so monumentally failed to realise his foolishness. Finally it was all just too much for him and he burst into tears, crying, "Oh! Oh! I will never be able to answer the question. For I realise now that I am not nearly clever enough to understand the secret of life."

"Now, now Thirsty Horse." said the teacher with genuine kindness in his voice. "This is not a moment to cry but rather a moment to be happy. Because even though you do not know the answer to your question, you have at least found out your mistake and so you are better off than you were before. But now let us help you with your question for it is very interesting for the whole class. And if we all consider it carefully and then discuss it together, then perhaps we will be able to understand it well enough to provide an answer?"

So for quite a long time after that the whole class discussed together Thirsty Horse's question "What is the secret of life?"; and of course, more than a little of the rest of Thirsty Horse's story as well. While since it was indeed a very interesting question that he had presented, there were many good ideas that it stimulated in response.

When finally the discussion was exhausted, the teacher summed up their conclusion, and this is what he said, "Thirsty Horse. First of all you should not be disheartened by the question that you face. The Cup of Curiosity set you this question to answer and so I do not think that it is beyond your powers to answer it. For if it were, then there would be no point in your search for that answer and the question would be no more than a trick, and it does not seem to me that it was the intention of the Cup to trick you. But even so, perhaps there are many answers to your question, and perhaps, too, every one of us at some time in his life must answer this same question for himself, in his own way and according to the lessons that his life teaches to him."

Now such was the power of this wisdom that as Thirsty Horse listened to his teacher speak he felt a new maturity enter his heart that he had not known before. He realised, too, that whatever he had thought in his moment of panic he was not stupid and that gave him a new confidence as well. While what is more, he had now finished his lessons at the school and trained his mind to answer questions even such as this. So finally he believed in his education and he believed in the value of his trained mind, and these things he added to what he had always believed in – the courage that he found in his heart.

...

When finally the time came for Thirsty Horse to leave the school and the town as well, no one would let him go without a farewell party. While Thirsty Horse could not leave without holding a last concert, and so all agreed that both should be held at once to make for the grandest celebration that could possibly be held.

Thirsty Horse gave the concert to say goodbye to his school and his friends, and since he wanted most to remember the times past and not the future to come, he played only the morin khuur. The guitar was not absent, though. For Music Maker came to the party and played that in accompaniment to Thirsty Horse, and the two instruments together sounded so sweetly beautiful as to make not just Thirsty Horse, this time, but everyone else cry too.

When the concert was over and before the party had gained too much momentum, the teacher took a moment to speak seriously and said, "Thirsty Horse, I will be sorry to see you go. But you have finished your schooling now, and I know in my heart that it is time for you to leave our little town."

Now after all the surprises that Thirsty Horse had encountered since he first decided to leave the herd and search for the end of the steppe, nothing had ever surprised him more than when he heard these words from his teacher. In fact so surprised was he that he almost jumped with amazement, which was very much to the surprise of his teacher as well. But once Thirsty Horse had recovered from his shock he asked a question that rather explained his reaction.

"Teacher, do you mean that there are towns that are even bigger than this one? For when first I came here, I doubted that even in a lifetime I would be able to walk down all its roads and streets and know them all, each to another. And even though we have studied cities in school, I never thought that they would really be bigger than our town here."

Then the teacher smiled, because he was actually very pleased that even though Thirsty Horse had certainly gained an education, he had not lost the simple sincerity of his character. But he made no comment on this as he replied, "And now, Thirsty Horse. Do you know all the roads and streets of our town and where they are, each to another?"

So Thirsty Horse thought for a while, and he thought for a while, and then he said, "Yes!" and there was quite some surprise in his voice as he spoke. For in fact it was a long time since he had learnt every foot and every corner of every road and street of the town. Yet it was not until this moment when the question was asked of him, that he finally realised that it was so.

...

Part 2

*In which
Thirsty Horse leaves
the school on the edge of the
steppe and travels the world
in search of an answer
to the question of the
Cup of Curiosity,*

"What is the secret of life."

Chapter 7:
The Great Earth Beneath the Stars

Before Thirsty Horse set out upon the next stage of his search for the secret of life, he asked his teacher if he had any suggestions as to which would be the best way to go; and he was rather pleased with the response.

"Considering the question of the Cup of Curiosity that you must answer," replied the teacher, "the route you choose to follow is something that requires careful consideration indeed. For what you really seek, Thirsty Horse, if you think about it, is a journey that will show you all the faces of the world."

"Indeed it is." agreed Thirsty Horse, nodding in wise acknowledgement of this fact.

So the teacher thought for a while, and then advised, "If I were you, Thirsty Horse, I would go first to the north-west while the summer weather lasts. There, if you go far enough, you will find a great lake and that will show you such a vast expanse of water that perhaps you will be able to imagine the sea that you have learnt of in class. You should know that this lake is nothing by comparison really. But once a lake reaches such a size that its far shore lies beyond the horizon and you cannot see how wide it is, then to your eyes it will at least appear as the sea. Only remember, so that you will understand, that it does not have the same heart, and therefore neither does it have the same passions, as the sea itself. But certainly it would be a good place to go first.

"Now obviously," continued the teacher, "you will take with you a map as detailed as you can find."

"But! - Yes!" Thirsty Horse wondered how it could be that the thought had not occurred to him. He had still to learn, he suddenly realised, how to put his education to practical use. "Obviously I will." he confirmed.

"Good." said the teacher. "Now it will take you about two months of walking to reach the lake, but the journey will take you a lot longer than that for what would be the point of it if you do not stop sometimes along the way. So I think that you will feel the winter approaching before you arrive; and it will be that, I believe, that will hurry you, finally, to your destination. Once you have arrived you will find fishermen by the lake and no doubt they will offer you the shelter of their homes. If I were you I would stay the rest of the winter with them. For on the one hand it will be too cold for travelling by then, while on the other hand you may learn from them their ways and perhaps the answer to your question too, if you are lucky.

"Once the sun begins to return and melt the snow, then you should leave the lake and go due south, using the sun to find your direction since at noon of each day you should be walking directly towards it. If you follow that course for the same distance again as it is from here to the lake, then you will cross first the steppe, then the Khangai Mountains, and then the Gobi Altai Mountains. This time, though, it will take you more than two months of walking because to this time you must add another month for the crossing of the mountains, which is a hard journey to make. Yet it will be worthwhile for the mountains will add to your adventures and your experiences another dimension of the world for you to understand.

"Once you have crossed the mountains you will find the steppe once again, and on the other side of that another range of mountains. Cross these mountains, though, and then you will find the great Gobi Desert, which is a dry wilderness and a very wild place indeed. There you must be very careful, for it is a harsh and dangerous terrain and home to many wild beasts, some of which are more ferocious even than wolves. But yet again it will be a worthwhile journey to make, for again it will show you another face of the world for you to understand – and perhaps it will even show you something more than itself. For they say that there is no more profound solitude on earth, nor any greater peace for any man, than he will find in a desert.

I have heard this many times and I believe it, although I must confess that I have never been there myself to know for sure. But I think that once you have passed all that distance to arrive in the desert, then perhaps it will be there, after all, that you will know the answer to your question. Because if it should be that you find your answer along the way but do not recognise it, perhaps the desert will give you a vision clear enough to see what you have missed before.

There the teacher paused for a moment - and he sighed. Because in his foretelling of this journey and the saying of these names, he had performed an evocation of places that for himself he had never seen - but yet of which he dreamed.

"The further you go into the desert," he eventually continued, "the harsher the desert will become – but it does not go on forever. If you can cross it all the way to the other side then you will be in China – and there you will find people indeed. But you will not be able to understand them since you do not speak their language - and that will be another problem for you to solve. Whether you cross the desert or not, though, is up to you; and I think that the moment itself will hold the decision that you make. But I am sure that you will make it that far at least."

From there you will still have to walk back and keep your rendezvous with the Cup of Curiosity – and that you must not forget. For it seems to me that the Cup will find you on the stated day wherever you are; and if you are not in the right place at that time, then it will be the worse for you to have broken the arrangement. You must go towards the north-east to make your return and the journey will take you another three months of walking, plus whatever time you pass along the way.

"If you follow this route and you stop along the way from time to time to ask your question, then it is quite possible that the whole journey, from this day until its end, will take you three years, which is all the time you have. Indeed I think you should be careful that it does not take you more. By the time you return to your rendezvous with the Cup of Curiosity, you will have known steppe, and lake, and mountain, and desert. You will have known and lived amongst all the people that you meet along the way, and you will have asked your question as many times as you will. So I think that by the time you finish this journey you will have found the answer to your question if it is possible for you to find it at all – and I believe that it is.

"Now the only other thing that I have to say to you Thirsty Horse," said the teacher, " - is Good Luck."

Now Thirsty Horse had listened very attentively to all of this and he concluded, quite correctly I would say, that this was indeed a good plan and that he would never think of a better one. So in his usual manner when it seemed to him that something explained was sincere and could be relied upon, he replied simply, "Thank you Teacher. Then that is the route that I shall follow."

"Then I am honoured that you have so graciously accepted my advice." said the teacher. "And I would have been honoured too," he continued, "to have given you, as a parting present, a map of mine that I think would serve you well. But as you have already thought of this need, then probably you already have …"

"No, no!" Thirsty Horse interrupted quickly. "I would be most honoured to accept your gift, teacher. Most honoured indeed, do not doubt."

So the teacher took from his pocket a large and neatly folded map which he handed to Thirsty Horse; and he smiled too as he did so. For he had guessed that the gift might really be welcome and why; and it amused him just a little to know that he had been right.

...

Everyone was sorry to see Thirsty Horse go. For within the boundaries of all they knew, from frontier to frontier of their town, Thirsty Horse, by nothing more than the goodness of his heart and the simple fact of trying so hard, had changed all of their lives for the better.

"And it seems to me," thought the teacher to himself, "that now he goes with no more and no less than that - to change the world."

...

As for Thirsty Horse himself, it was a sad moment for him too, to leave the town after having been so happy there for so long; and indeed after having achieved so much while he was there. Yet leave he had to do, for his destiny no longer held him to the place but called him elsewhere.

The hardest part of leaving was to take the first step. But once he had begun he put his head down and he just kept walking. Then once he was beyond the frontier of the town he kept walking for perhaps an hour before he stopped and looked back, and he expected to feel sad when he did. Yet to his surprise he did not feel sad at all, but rather his heart suddenly leapt for joy at the sight of the town in the distance and he knew this moment to be right. For he had given to the town as much as the town had given to him and at the end of that time each had left the other free to follow his destiny when it called; and that was a successful partnership indeed.

"And who knows, perhaps I shall return one day?" said Thirsty Horse aloud as he stood alone upon the open steppe and looked towards the town. "For now that I have my freedom I know of no reason why I should not."

...

Now something that Thirsty Horse discovered very quickly when he began this new journey, and which was rather to his surprise, was that he was no longer as fit as he had been before. In truth he was still very fit. But after a year of living comfortably in the town and sitting for so many hours each day in the school to learn, he did not have quite the excellence of physical condition that he had boasted before. During the first week or two of his journey, therefore, he found the walking to be rather tougher than he had expected. But after that he found his form again and the journey became easier, as he was rather hoping it would.

So Thirsty Horse travelled upon the open steppe once more. He made good time while he walked, and just as he had done before he stopped whenever he came upon people and he played the guitar for them in return for their hospitality, their food and their company. When there was no one to play for he camped out upon the open steppe and he counted again the gifts of the stars to men; for once again the stars revealed to him their gifts - just as they had done before.

...

Now one night during this particular journey, when Thirsty Horse was alone upon the steppe, he suddenly began to feel very lonely, which was unusual for him since he was normally content to be alone and to look forward to the pleasure of his next meeting. Yet something, this time - some new revelation, was nagging at his mind - although he just could not quite work out what it was.

Of course there was nothing better for him to do, while he found himself in the grip of this enigmatic mood of depression, than to take his guitar and attempt to exorcise it with music; and so that is what he did. But then he found it strange that the song that came to him was a melancholy lament for the open steppe, since that is where he was.

When a little while later he realised how much he wanted to run once more as a horse upon that open steppe, it seemed to Thirsty Horse that he had found the answer to his strange mood. But he continued to play, and he left the music to indulge his thoughts and feelings as it would while he awaited the relieve of his heart. Yet still this strange mood would not lift!

So Thirsty Horse looked up to the stars and said, "I will play on, and I hope that you like my playing. If you do, then perhaps when I finish my song you will tell me the meaning of this strange inspiration that you have put within my heart."

It was a very long and sonorous piece that Thirsty Horse played; and he played it with feeling and conviction and made no mistakes at all right to the very last note. Then when he had finished he found that his mood was no longer one of loneliness that he did not understand, but had changed to a feeling of calm and satisfying accomplishment. So it seemed to him that the stars had indeed been pleased with his playing and he looked up to see if they agreed. As he gazed upwards he remembered that first night when he had left the herd, and how he had run so far through the darkness with only the light of the moon to show him the way: a full moon that had shone to show the way to a horse who ran in search of the end of the steppe. While on this night there was no moon and all the light he had was cast by the stars or by the fire that he had made himself - and it was then that Thirsty Horse suddenly knew the meaning of the strange inspiration that had come to him this night! For even though he had reached the edge of the steppe when he had found the town and the school, it was only now that he realised what that meant within his heart.

As for where he journeyed now, he had to think about that for a while. But then like so many things that Thirsty Horse had learned by inspiration while he camped upon the open steppe, the answer came to him in the same way. And what the inspiration taught him, this time, was that now he was freed from the limitations of the steppe - he journeyed upon all of the Great Earth that lay beneath the Stars.

...

When Thirsty Horse awoke the next day, he knew exactly what he wanted to do. So he used the second of his wishes to become a horse again. Then he ran for all he was worth, and all the while he ran he thought about how simple life had been when there had been no question of the secret of life to be answered. When all he had to do was to reach the edge of the steppe - and to run faster than the wolves.

...

The Thirsty Horse of Mongolia

Chapter 8:
Journeys Yet to Come.

It was indeed a very long way to the Khovskul Lake and finally it took four months before Thirsty Horse came to its shores and the camps of the fishermen who live there. Very glad he was to arrive too, for by now there was a thin mantle of snow glistening upon the ground all around and the nights out upon the open steppe, with the temperatures falling as low as minus twenty degrees, were becoming dangerously cold. So it was that by the time Thirsty Horse enquired, shivering, within the first habitation that he came to, he was more than grateful to be given shelter and warmth inside.

The people by the lake were just as friendly as Thirsty Horse usually found people to be and he was happy to stay with them for the winter. Yet he had travelled a very long way now from the steppe where his journey had begun and the land had changed along the way, while in consequence the people had changed too. To begin with they did not live in gers, but rather in tents. These they made from long wooden poles that were set in the ground, inclined towards each other and tied at the top to form an inverted cone, and then draped over with animal skins. The animals they tended were different too and of a kind that Thirsty Horse had never seen before - they were reindeer.

Not only did these people live differently, but they had different memories and told different stories too. So Thirsty Horse would sit with his hosts in the evenings after their work was done and listen in fascination while they told of their life and their history by the shores of the lake. While in addition to these stories they would tell of legends ' and fables from the great land to the North and it was to these mysteries that he listened in deepest rapture. Stories from the land of Siberia, as it was called, which in winter was even colder than Mongolia, hard though it was for Thirsty Horse to believe that possible! But they said it was; and they told him too that in winter, in the far north of that land, the sun never came at all. While in summertime it never set but rather left its light to play upon the northern ice cap of the world and send wave upon wave of multicoloured light shooting up into the sky - and that for no other reason than for the beauty of the sight. Really this was a story to enthral if ever there was on; and to Thirsty Horse the material upon which to build his dreams of the future yet to come.

"Perhaps one day," he thought to himself, "I will go there and see these wonders for myself." For it must be said that already the Great Earth called him to go and his heart would never again be able to rest until his footsteps had measured all the miles of the journey and the memory of it had been written upon his soul.

In return for their stories, Thirsty Horse played the guitar and sang to amuse his hosts - and he played and sang as well as he could for he thought himself well paid for his trouble. While since he had time as much as they to use during the day, he put himself to other uses as well. Sometimes he helped them out with their work; but mostly what he did was to repeat to their children, and whoever else might care to listen, the lessons that he had learned in school.

Now in the giving of these lessons Thirsty Horse found a new pleasure and a satisfaction that went far beyond his expectations. For suddenly he was privileged to watch the faces of children while their minds were taken, teased and challenged, by new ideas that had previously lain beyond their imaginations. It was a great satisfaction indeed; yet Thirsty Horse could not help but realise too the responsibility that lay beyond the pleasure that he took. For would not his own morality be offended if he were just to pass on by, keeping his knowledge to himself and leaving these children to continue their lives in ignorance of all he knew?

...

Very often during this winter time Thirsty Horse would stand on the shore of Khovskul Lake, and remembering the words of his teacher he would try to imagine the sea. From its shores, the lake appeared as a great desert of water that stretched to the horizon - and how far beyond that he had no idea, just as his teacher had said. Indeed the lake did appear as he believed the sea to be - except that the sea would not be so calm, he had learned in school. So he tried to imagine waves breaking upon the shore; and he tried too, to imagine a sea breeze blowing and the smell of salt water; water that ran so deep that even the sun had not the power to penetrate its depths. He tried very hard to imagine all of this. Yet finally he had to admit, which was very much to his disappointment, that it simply defied his imagination to conjure up such details within his mind.

When he thought about the ocean he remembered that it was so big, in fact, that it covered nearly twice the area of all the land that this planet held. While all the land that he had travelled was just a very small part of even that. He remembered too that the sea guarded within its depths not only the deepest trenches of the earth but also the highest mountains, and yet even they did not climb high enough to reach the surface of its waters. He tried to imagine the deep places of the oceans that no man had ever seen, and within his mind alone to see their mysteries, of which men knew even less than they did of the surface of the moon.

In this way Thirsty Horse tried to imagine the sea while he gazed upon Khovskul Lake and with all the power of his mind he concentrated upon that greatest legend of the Great Earth. Yet when he looked away he realised that all he knew was Khovskul Lake and the only comforting thought he could take from all his imaginings was this. That such was the mystery of the sea that even if he had gazed upon its surface, still he would not have known any more of it than that.

"But one day," he thought, "I would like to gaze upon its surface nonetheless."

...

While the winter drew out and the days slowly lengthened towards spring, Thirsty Horse stayed with the people by the lake and he learnt their ways: of fishing and of tending their animals; of building and repairing their homes, and of running their lives in general.

Sometimes, when it seemed that the moment was right, he would ask of someone, if the person gave the impression that he might know, "Please kind Sir," or he would say Madame if it were the case, "but can you tell me the secret of life?"

Now once Thirsty Horse had asked this question twenty times or so, he was rather surprised to discover that nobody seemed to have really very much of an idea at all of how to answer it. Then it crossed his mind to wonder that if nobody knew the answer, then why did he need to know it himself? For surely the Cup of Curiosity would not turn all the men there were into horses if they could not answer the question? While since so many obviously could not, then perhaps there was a clue in that as to the answer itself. Perhaps, indeed, it was a clue to the fact that - there was no answer?

Now it may have been a strange coincidence, but just as Thirsty Horse was thinking this very thing he happened, quite by chance, to meet a man who was passing along the shore of the lake. This man was the only person that he ever met by the lake who did give him an answer to his question, while the answer that the man gave was really much the same as this answer that Thirsty Horse was thinking at the

time. Of course the whole conversation was rather more complicated, and it went something like this:

"Please kind Sir." Thirsty Horse asked the man, "but I wonder if you may be able to help me? You see, I am trying to find the secret of life and I have asked this question of all whom I have met so far in my life as a boy. Yet no one seems to have the least idea of how to answer it – not the least idea at all, in fact! Now do you not find that strange?"

"Not really." replied the man with barely even a hesitation. "For their lack of answers may be considered in another way." Then the man began his explanation like this, "Consider, my young friend, that for each person that you meet by the lake his life makes sense, and that means that he does, in his heart, know why. Then consider, too, that he does not ask himself your question and why he does not?

"Now I will tell you why. It is because the people who live by the lake, like most people everywhere in fact, have no need to ask such a question in order for their lives to make sense. Why they cannot tell you that, of course, is simply because it is something that they all understand of each other and so they have no need to express such thoughts in words."

Now here, thought Thirsty Horse to himself, was a man gifted in the powers of analysis; and one too who might very likely reveal the secret of life - with just a little more prompting on the subject? For indeed he seemed to be coming very close to explaining it already.

"Very interesting," replied Thirsty Horse thoughtfully, "and quite possibly you are right." he added with considerable optimism. Yet still he thought about what the man had said for a little while longer without comment, for somehow he was not quite satisfied yet. When he had finally managed to muster his thoughts together, he asked, "But to turn your explanation another way, kind Sir, surely it cannot be that just because no one has ever formulated the answer in words, it cannot be so expressed. While since I do seek the answer, and must in the course of my future explain it to another - who is not here now to see this wisdom for himself, then for me it is necessary to formulate this answer in words. So perhaps, kind Sir, you could help me with this task?"

Then the man thought for a while in his turn before he answered, "Since you have need, young friend, then so it shall be."

So the man thought for a while more, while Thirsty Horse waited patiently. Then he gave to Thirsty Horse the secret of life, as he understood it to be, in these words, "People live and work and do not stop to ask themselves why," he began, "because all that happens will happen anyway, no matter what they do to try and change it. They have realised, indeed, that all is written down by destiny and nothing can ever be changed, while to fight against it is simply to suffer. How much better, therefore, to have the wisdom to do nothing - and graciously to accept your fate."

Then the man smiled and looked to be rather satisfied with his explanation, which indeed he was. So he drew a deep breath and gave to it this benediction, "Yes, my young friend. That, indeed, is the secret of life."

"Hmm!" said Thirsty Horse at this. For although he could certainly appreciate the wisdom and coherence of this explanation, he could not say of himself that he was entirely satisfied with it. Certainly it did seem to make some sense to him, and indeed it caused him to think very carefully upon this theme for quite some time. But finally he was not convinced, and finally he knew why.

"I can understand, kind Sir," began Thirsty Horse in his reply, "that a man may think like that. For a man may think in many strange and wonderful ways and still understand the meaning within his abstractions. But a horse is an animal dear to my heart and also very influential to my way of thinking, although I will not trouble you now as to why that is. Yet since it is, I cannot help myself from considering your explanation from the point of view of a horse. Now a horse, whose life is very simple and whose mind is not so frequently given to such wondrous exercises in thought, cannot escape the simplest of wisdom that life has to teach. So a horse may often be faced with a simple choice of whether to run from a pack of hungry wolves, for instance, or stand and die to let them fill their bellies. And you may take it from me that at such times as that a horse does not dwell for very long upon the thought that perhaps he cannot, by his actions, change his destiny. In fact, and to put it bluntly, he knows perfectly well that his destiny will be dictated by nothing more than the speed at which he can run - and a little bit of luck that certainly warrants no grander name. But for him there is no destiny that cares not either way and he knows full well that he lives, or dies, by his own choice. Now if that is true for horses, who are really quite simple animals, then how much more must it be true for men? For men have the ability to change what is around them far more than the horses can ever do.

"So no, kind sir." Thirsty Horse continued. "I do indeed thank you for your answer and I congratulate you too on the admirable way in which you so logically analysed and presented it. Yet I must conclude, kind sir, that the answer which you give – is not the secret of life."

Now this rejection by Thirsty Horse was made in such praising tones that the man simply could not be offended by it - yet still he wished to defend his point of view. For being, as he was, considerably older than his interlocutor, he could not, for reasons of social hierarchy, reasonably accept to have been proved wrong. So the man smiled politely at Thirsty Horse and said, "I am sorry, my young friend, but I think you have taken my answer rather too simply to really understand its meaning. Perhaps when you are older you will consider it again, and then understand it better."

Now Thirsty Horse was usually very polite to all he met. Yet for some reason this argument of the man, with its fatalistic pessimism, had provoked in him, and for the first time in his life, nothing less than a youthful belligerence and a desire to argue back. So Thirsty Horse quite forcefully defended himself now, although still not wishing to offend – but then again not caring too much if he did, "Perhaps you are right, kind sir, that I have understood your answer in too simple terms. But then it seems to me at least," he said curtly, "that the key to revealing its flaw, lies in seeing it as simply as that."

"Hmm." said the man, and at this he looked somewhat less amused.

Then neither of them spoke for a while, until both concluded that it would be best to finish their discussion there and so that is what they did. As for Thirsty Horse, he never bothered to consider this line of logic again and he never regretted either that he did not.

...

When the spring finally arrived, Thirsty Horse was pleased to go once again on his way, although he was sorry to say good bye to all the friends that he had made as well as to the children and other people who he had taught.

He took one last morning to say his farewells, and he had good reason for that. Because at midday exactly when he looked up to the sun it gave him his direction of due south and he started to walk towards it,. Then he continued to walk in a dead straight line while the sun fell slowly from the sky towards the horizon to his right.

He did not walk so far that first day. Yet by the time he stopped and looked back he could no longer see the shores of the Lake nor the dwellings of the people whose stories and whose hospitality he had so enjoyed. So he knew then that he had walked far enough to be once again upon the road of his destiny and to have left behind him Khovskul Lake: the furthest point north that he would travel on this journey of his life.

Thirsty Horse knew too that in just the space of that afternoon he had travelled already too far to turn back. While in his heart he was happy with the memories he took with him: of times past with friends together, whether cold days of work or warm evenings of good company by glowing fires; of things learnt and things shared; and of occasions celebrated that deserved to be. But still what he valued most from this time spent by the Khovskul Lake, were the tales from beyond its frontiers that its people had told, and the future that these tales had left for him to dream.

...

Chapter 9:
Into the Realm of the Eagles

The land south of Khovskul Lake was sparsely forested and scattered with low mountains, which Thirsty Horse skirted around when they stood in this way. Soon he picked up the course of the river that ran into the lake from the south; and since he had checked its course upon his map and knew that it too came from the direction he wished to follow, follow it is what he did.

He soon found that there were other benefits as well from following the course of the river, such as being able to travel light without the need to carry water with him. While since there were many trees in this area, and many close to the river particularly, neither did he need to carry with him wood for his fire at night.

This section of the river was not so remote as many places that Thirsty Horse had travelled and so there would usually be a path along the river bank, made by the men and animals that used the way. For the river provided water to drink and fish to eat and many were drawn to benefit from its offerings, just as Thirsty Horse was grateful to benefit too.

So Thirsty Horse followed the course of the river, while he watched its twists and turns and thought about these things; and sometimes too he would sit by its banks and rest for a while just watching its waters flow. Just considering how it picked its way between hills and mountains and followed the contours of the land until it arrived, eventually, at a great, empty bowl of the earth and poured within. Poured and poured and poured, in fact, until it had completely filled the bowl and made - the great Khovskul Lake; and that the fulfilment of its destiny. That is how Thirsty Horse came to appreciate the river for what it was, and to understand the journey that it made to cross the land. Now would his own destiny, he wondered, ever be so well fulfilled as that?

Once the river turned to the east, Thirsty Horse left its course and continued due south by the sun, threading his way through the mountains by his own decision - and of course, that marked the difference in their destinies too.

This route of keeping to the lower ground was not only the least tiring, but it also led him to meet the largest number of people. The latter fact being most fortuitous since Thirsty Horse still relied upon the trade of music in exchange for food; and as much too, to gain from his conversations with the people whom he met. He didn't find the answer to his question, though, and he learned nothing of any particular note - although he did hear some interesting stories along the way.

All in all it was a good time to make this journey along this easy path across open land with trees and low mountains scattered here and there. A land that provided wood for a fire at night and displayed such soft and pleasing contours as made of the landscape a prettier picture beneath the sun. While a warm breeze blew each day to bring the promise of summer; and Thirsty Horse played his guitar with a feeling of simple happiness within his heart. Then in the cool airs of each night he slept easy beneath the stars; and each day the sun rose higher in the sky to make the tasks that came with the new dawn just a little easier than those of the last.

...

Thirsty Horse walked on towards the sun until he came across another river, which he knew from his map he could follow around the first rise of the Khangai mountains that stood before him now. Following the river further on the map he saw that he could in fact, if he wanted, follow its course all the way around the lower mountains of the Khangai and eventually to a pass between its highest peaks. By following this course he could avoid completely the crossing of the mountains and all the hardship that would come with it - and therein lay his dilemma. For tempting as it was to take the easier route, Thirsty Horse had not set out upon this journey with the intention of avoiding the lessons that the miles had to teach. So finally he looked up at the sun, and then deciding where his direction lay, continued on his course due south and straight towards the highest peaks of the Khangai Range.

Once Thirsty Horse had crossed this second river, it proved to be very fortunate that he could, indeed, navigate by the sun. Since the northern slopes that he climbed now, although they were not so steep, were quite heavily forested; and only the sun was high enough in the sky to show him the way.

But there was more to learn from the forest than a gratitude for the height of the sun, as Thirsty Horse quickly came to understand. For in much the same way that he had never seen the sea, neither had he ever seen forests before; and as he passed between the trees he could not help his imagination from wondering nervously what might be hiding behind each one. It was similarly disconcerting that he could not see very far. Because any dangerous animal that felt so inclined would be able to hide behind the trees, or creep up behind him, without him knowing. On the open steppe when he could see clearly for miles his usual custom of looking around every now and again had served him well. But here in the trees he would have to be looking around constantly to stand any real chance of not being taken unawares – and that worried him. So Thirsty Horse went very cautiously through the trees and wondered with considerable apprehension what lessons he might be able to learn from this experience.

Now in truth, most of what Thirsty Horse did learn from this part of his journey was indeed the effect it had on his imagination. Yet there was, too, one practical lesson that it taught him. For in his fear at being surprised by some strange animal creeping up behind him, Thirsty Horse took to stopping very frequently and listening, and so he learned that where the eyes are of little use, the ears may serve better.

Since Thirsty Horse was a lot more comfortable on open ground than in the trees, he endeavoured each night to find a clearing where he could camp – and always he achieved this. Until one night, that is, when he found himself still deep in the forest's depths as the light faded and with no possibility of breaking cover before darkness!

Now this was a terrifying predicament indeed, for Thirsty Horse really had no desire to sleep in the forest. Yet he did not panic, but thought about this for a while – until finally he had an idea; which was to climb into the branches of a big tree, to tie himself in, and to sleep there – and so that is what he did. He slept lightly in the tree and he left some food on the ground a little distance away to distract any dangerous animal that might come along during the night.

So it was that Thirsty Horse was awakened from his light slumber that night by the grunting and shuffling of a very big bear that came past his tree, attracted indeed by the smell of the food. Now since bears do have a very good sense of smell it is quite possible that this one could have easily detected Thirsty Horse too while he hid in his tree. In was fortunate, therefore, that for this bear at least, Thirsty Horse's plan did work and he passed on by, distracted by the smell of the food on the ground. Perhaps it is difficult to smell something that is high up as well, which would have helped. But whichever it was, Thirsty Horse held his breath and remained completely still and silent as the bear passed by beneath him.

In the morning, Thirsty Horse came cautiously down from his tree to find that his diversion of food had been eaten and that the bear was long gone. Yet he wasn't particularly worried about this since in the presence of the bear he had felt safe in his tree, and finally, therefore, safe in the forest. So the lesson that he had learned from the forest was how to adapt and survive in this new and unfamiliar environment; and with that, at last, Thirsty Horse felt quite at ease.

He continued on through the forests and clearings of this country and he found that during the day the wildlife was plentiful indeed. He saw many eagles circling in the sky and often deer running across the clearing between the trees. Sometimes wild boar, and twice more – grizzly bear! But there his luck helped him out, for both times they were quite far away and he never came across them by surprise close to.

...

Once Thirsty Horse had made it to the far side of the forest he was properly in the high mountains of the Khangai Range and on terrain that he had never travelled before. While it wasn't until he actually started to climb that he realised how hard the crossing of the mountains would be. When he found out, it seemed to him that the challenge deserved considerably more by way of acknowledgement than his teacher had given it. Certainly more than, "Add a month to the journey for the crossing of the mountains." as he recalled it had been.

But his teacher had been right too in that the mountains would teach him their mysteries while he crossed them, and the lessons began with the very first footfall that he set to his ascent. For apart from the toughness of the climbing itself, there was also a remoteness to the land around him that even he, in all his travels, had never felt before and which weighed upon his senses now. While he wondered still, from time to time, what animals might possibly be waiting for him around each turn in the mountain's folds, and he took to checking a lot more carefully than he had before the tracks that crossed his path.

In this way he knew when there were wolves around, or bears, or mountains goats, or deer. While there was one animal in particular that he watched for and of which thoughts of its ferocity sometimes kept him awake at night. For it is not easy to sleep soundly alone in a land where wolverines come quickly to haunt your dreams.

Yet the forest had already taught Thirsty Horse the art of adapting to new situations and that he continued to do. He was careful to lay various warning devices around his camp, made from string and bits of wood or metal, that would sound if anything touched them; and he slept lightly enough that he would awake instantly if anything did. He would always leave his food, too, at some distance away from himself. So that if any animal did come by, it would be attracted to that first – just as the bear had been before, and which Thirsty Horse would know from his trip wires. But fortunately his luck held in the mountains and he was never awoken at night by anything more dangerous than a mountain goat.

As for people, Thirsty Horse had not expected to meet many people in the Khangai Range, and indeed in the high mountains and in the forests he met no one at all.

...

It wasn't until Thirsty Horse had reached the last peak of the range and could see clearly across all the land on the other side for as far as the clarity of the air and the curve of the earth would permit, that he had any idea at all of the sense of accomplishment that the end of his climb would bring him. But then suddenly the realisation of that achievement just hit him as a wave of euphoria breaking upon his

mind. A wave that he now realised had begun as a ripple unknown with the first footfall that he had set to the climb; then grown in size and strength without his knowing until it had reached the monumental proportions of this moment now when the wave broke with full force upon his mind. It was, perhaps, the most incredible sensation that Thirsty Horse had ever known and as great a reward as he could possibly have imagined for the effort of his climb. So he stayed for a while upon that last summit to savour the pleasure of that moment: to breathe it in and live it for as long as he wished it to last. Until, in fact, he could call himself content just to say that it had been worth it. Then Thirsty Horse set himself to descend and found the exercise to be a pleasure indeed as his feet fell easily to the descent and his lungs no longer strained for the oxygen that it took to climb.

Now as Thirsty Horse scrambled easily down the south facing slopes of the Khangai Range with a big grin on his face, another thought came to him that made him stop for a while and consider its value. It seemed to him that this thought was no less than the true lesson of the mountains and the reward of the Great Earth herself for the accomplishment of his task; and what he thought was this: that by dint of effort and perseverance, and by the application of all the gifts of the Stars that he possessed in the measure that they had given him, he, Thirsty Horse, had succeeded to reach and to stand upon the highest point in the world. Now if he could do that, then could he not, too, with no more than these same gifts and his own character, succeed in any task that his destiny set him? Could he not, indeed, even find the secret of life itself?

. . .

The great steppe of Eastern Mongolia runs in a huge curving swathe down from the north east of the country and into its final reaches between the Khangai and the Gobi Altai mountains - and it was here that Thirsty Horse found himself when he reached the end of his descent. Since it was, in fact, the last stretch of the very same steppe where Thirsty Horse had been born, you could truly say that now he had reached the end of the steppe, not only in his heart but beneath his feet as well. Yet the feeling that grew within him in this moment had little to do with this accomplishment. Here he had returned once more to the steppe of his childhood that he knew and understood better than any other land, nothing more or less in fact than the land he loved most, and he took a greater comfort from it now than ever he had before.

With this sentiment in his heart he did not hasten to cross this terrain, but took rather longer, in fact, than even a slow pace really required. He tarried for love of this land and he camped early each day to play his guitar for as many hours of each night as he could.

Such were the emotions of Thirsty Horse at this strangely distant homecoming that they led him, one night, to begin a new composition of his own, which it took him several days, in fact, to finish. Yet finally he did finish it and then he played the whole piece through many times. Each time savouring the sonorities of this "hymn to the steppe" that he had been inspired to compose; and each time varying his interpretation the more to explore its moods and its meaning.

...

When Thirsty Horse awoke the day after he had finished his composition, he looked up to the south and saw that the high mountains of the Gobi Altai Range were now quite close. Then he knew that he would reach the first of their slopes by the end of this day, and so this would be his last day upon the steppe. Yet he was not sad at this, for he had taken from the steppe its gift to him this time; and he knew that now he had the blessing of this land to move on.

On this last day of his crossing of the steppe he watched the great mountains of the Gobi Altai Range rise ever higher before him; and these mountains, he knew from his map, rose even higher than those of the Khangai. Yet he knew too that the range was no wider than one ridgeline and so to cross them, he mused, would not be so hard as the Khangai Range had been. It was then that the idea came to him, not just to cross these mountains, but to cross them by way of the highest peak that they offered in his path – and that stood at nearly 4,000m high.

...

Since he was now well practised in the climbing of mountains, Thirsty Horse did indeed make it to this highest peak; and he did indeed know once again the euphoria of accomplishment that he had known before. Truly it was a superb satisfaction that he felt, although it did not surprise him this second time around – while there was another experience of these mountains that certainly did.

After the loneliness of the Khangai, Thirsty Horse had no expectation at all of meeting another human being while crossing the heights of the Gobi Altai. Yet there was one man that he met in these mountains, and it was a meeting that he would remember well. For it was a meeting worthwhile indeed.

Thirsty Horse did not find the man, but rather the man found him – and jumped down suddenly from high on the rocks before him to bar his way, quite scaring him too. Yet Thirsty Horse was prepared for an attack sooner or later, whether from wolves or robbers or whatever else. So with the swiftest of practised movements and in less than an instant he had reached behind him to draw out his staff from where it rested across his back and brandish it menacingly before him.

"Who are you?" challenged Thirsty Horse staunchly.

"Aye, and who are you?" replied the man, "You boy, who come to cross this bare mountain alone! And is it from need and with the courage to dare that you come, or are you just mad and know no better?"

From this counter, Thirsty Horse understood that the man was not a robber, and was rather re-assured by this observation too. So he relaxed a little from his defensive stance and he replied simply and honestly, "I come from need upon a quest to answer a question. Although as to where I will find the answer to my question, that I do not know – save to think that once I have seen all the faces of the world in my search, then perhaps I will know it from the journey itself."

Now it must be said that the man was rather surprised when he heard this from Thirsty Horse, indeed who would not be? So he thought for a while before he said, "Is that so, boy. Then tell me - what is your question?"

"My question," replied Thirsty Horse, "is, what is the secret of life?"

At this the man smiled and said, "Aye, boy. I think you may be right. For if you journey across the world until you have seen all its faces and that does not teach you the answer, then what else is there that will?"

"Only the men that I meet along the way." replied Thirsty Horse. "Perhaps they will know."

At which the man looked rather shocked. But he recovered quickly, and he replied in his dour voice, "Aye, perhaps they will; and perhaps from them you will know it, although for that you will have to trust what they say – and that's more than I'd do myself."

Of course when Thirsty Horse heard this, he thought to himself that this man was more than usually suspicious of others, to say the least. But then again that was hardly surprising in one who chose, apparently, to spend his life in solitude upon a mountain as lonely as this. For unlike Thirsty Horse the man did not appear to be engaged in crossing the mountain at all, but rather gave the impression that he was there because that is where he most wanted to be.

Yet whatever the differences may have been in their reasons for being on this mountain at the same time, they had both been led by their characters and their destinies to this moment and this meeting. So perhaps it wasn't so surprising either that they fell into conversation together, or that the conversation proved to be interesting and satisfying for them both.

Now in this meeting with this strange and enigmatic character, Thirsty Horse judged that he had come across a rare chance indeed to ask his question of one whose experience was far from the ordinary. While he hoped, too, to receive an answer that lived up to his assessment of the man. So after they had passed some time in talking amiably together, Thirsty Horse judged the moment to be right and he said to the man, "Even from your face I can see that your life has led you to many experiences - and those very different from mine I would guess. So although you did not offer an answer when I told you my question first, still it seems to me that perhaps you know. So please tell me if you can, from your own experiences - what is the secret of life?"

Then the man scratched his head for a while and looked a little awkward before he replied, "That, boy, I do not know. At least not beyond what it is to be alive and to be free and to live as you please. I don't know so much for its secret, as ye say, but that for me is life itself - and if I am denied that liberty, then there is nothing else for me but to fight until I win it back – or die in the attempt if I must."

Then the man thought about his words for a little longer still, while Thirsty Horse waited silently and patiently. For he knew that the man was considering this question in a way that he never had before - and that he needed, therefore, an appropriate length of time for such reflection.

Finally the man confirmed, "Aye, that is my creed, boy – and if ye wish to tell it that way, ye can say from me that that is the secret of life, at least as best as I know it to be."

Then the man ceased from his thoughts and looked very seriously at Thirsty Horse as he said, "But the secret of life is your business, boy, and for myself I've never had need to ask that question. Other things, though, I do know; and many of those have been just as hard in the learning as the answer that you seek now will probably be. But I'll tell ye, boy, if ye'll listen, of things that may help ye on your way. For I like you, boy – and to help you if I can would be my pleasure."

After this introduction the man continued, and Thirsty Horse could see in his eyes the depth of his sincerity as he spoke, "Aye, 'tis true as ye say, boy, that perhaps ye will hear what ye seek from the mouths of men. But never be quick to trust what ye hear, for the tongues of men are not so often adept to the truth and usually would rather twist it to their own ends if they can.

"Now ye can guess, boy, that I've no time for such as those – and that's why I choose to live on this mountain where none of their like will ever come. While if I do sometimes wish for company, and that perhaps I do, then it is for the company of men of my own mind that I wish. Men who would dare, you'll understand, to come here to this mountain. While as to that - no one ever has but you."

Then the man gave Thirsty Horse a look of fondness that came spontaneously to this friendship so newly begun, and said, "Aye, you've a strong heart boy, whether ye know it yet or not, and I'll tell ye too what that means, 'though you'll learn it for yourself soon enough.

"To be free and to believe no one before judging for yourself their words by the counsel of your own heart, that is what it means boy. For in his heart each man will always know the truth - but the questions I ask are these: will he be good enough in his character to listen to it, boy? And will he be strong enough to accept it if he does? Or will he even want to try? For there are all kinds of men in the world and not so many of them as you might believe ever hold themselves so proud. As to why that should be? I say it is because they stop to ask themselves for what it serves to think? What gain it brings to make your own decision and accept the responsibility for that, when orders can be followed and the deaths of innocents lain before the feet of another - who yet did not do the deed? And finally because they conclude that it is best in this world to follow the easiest path to riches and their own satisfaction, caring not for what is in their hearts at all!

"And are they not right, boy? When I, who disagree, have nothing to show for my disagreement except that I stand here now upon this mountain alone."

There the man finished his proclamation upon the mountain's peak, yet he did not finish it well enough for Thirsty Horse, who added this,

"No, they are wrong - those who do not listen to their hearts. For beneath the Stars that shine above steppe and mountain alike; that grant to men the gifts they use to make their lives and their world; that set the truth and judge it in us all – they are wrong."

Now when he heard these words the man gave Thirsty Horse such a look that a whole ocean of sadness and respect was marked upon his face; and then he said in a voice most tender to hear,

"Aye, ye're a boy for foolish deeds, and that's for sure. But that is for your courage I see, and your courage touches my heart. So I'll tell ye, boy, that on this day I'll count anew the number of men who hold my respect. I count from the living, boy, and I tell ye straight, my count is one."

Then so moved was Thirsty Horse by the gravity of this sentiment and the magnitude of this complement to himself that he actually reeled under the shock. When he had recovered, though, he duly responded as best he could, "By your complement I am deeply honoured - and more so, in fact, than I could ever deserve. But as for the rest of men, there are others that I could introduce to you who would change your opinion I am sure."

"Aye, boy, perhaps you could." the man replied. "But for myself, my destiny has not led me to find such men while of others I have learned very well indeed - and the scar of that, boy, is that my heart no longer believes in my own kind nor even seeks their company any more. But still I'll thank my destiny, and you boy, for this one thing. That I will go from this meeting with no more hatred in my heart for what is past."

At the end of this conversation, Thirsty Horse did not ask the man for the story of his life, although he knew him now for a soldier all the same. His reply was simply this, "Then I am glad too that my destiny has led me to achieve this service to you. For that alone was worth the crossing of this mountain a thousand times or more."

...

When he reached the last ridge and crossed it, Thirsty Horse found that in the clear mountain air he could see so far that it seemed to the end of the world; and what he saw was the great Gobi Desert, just as his teacher had said he would. Out across the land and even beyond the far horizon so many miles away, it seemed to go on forever. While from his high perch within the mountains' grasp this sight was so new and strange to Thirsty Horse that it made his heart bound with pleasure at the sight. Then he wondered what new miracles the desert would show that perhaps would be even stranger than all that had passed before.

...

Chapter 10:
The Great Han Khan

Such was the shape of the last mountain that its slopes never lost their steepness even when they reached the desert floor, but rather disappeared sheer beneath the ruffle of the desert's skirts as they billowed wide to trespass upon the mountain's feet. This arrogance of the desert was displayed with neither explanation nor apology, being just the power of the new world in its rightful place, claiming its own. Yet still it was a sudden shock of transition between one world and the next and it struck Thirsty Horse like a thunder bolt of change when finally he took that last step between the two. For to him it was the future foreseen now achieved: enough to leave him awed and silent before its dawn, wondering why his destiny had brought him here and what he should do now. But then, now that he had crossed steppe and mountain and steppe and mountain again, what else really could he think to do with this desert than to cross it in its turn? So it will come as no surprise to know that that is what he set out to do; nor that he hoped, not just to reach its other side, but in so doing to learn from the desert its secrets and its wonders too.

To be accurate, it was not true desert that stretched before him now but rather a desertic steppe. A vast and desolate land of extreme winter cold or summer heat that was barren enough to be called a desert. Yet still was blessed, nevertheless, with enough scrub vegetation, at least from time to time, to sustain any animal tough enough to survive its humour; and there was water too – if you could find it that is. Now this leads to a point of rather practical concern that should be noted here. For whether there was water or not it is still to be appreciated that here there was certainly no such thing as a plentiful supply. So the point of practical concern was simply this, that by the time Thirsty Horse made it all the way down from the mountains he was being hurried on his way by winter's threat to freeze his heels to the rock if he tarried. Yet if he had been lucky to be quick enough out of the mountains in this season, he was also lucky not to be too quick. For in as much as it was the December snows that finally chased him out, it was they, too, who having failed to kill him as they had threatened, then measured their respect for his victory by filling his water bottles with as much water as he could carry. In fact it was only that, and the cold in the desert itself which would not rob him too much of his precious water, that made of the crossing of the desertic steppe and the true desert beyond a possibility at all.

With as much water as he could carry and the map that his teacher had given him clutched firmly in his hand like a charm for luck that went well beyond its use, Thirsty Horse wrapped his winter coat tight around him and his scarf across his face. Then just as he had done since on every day since he left the great lake, he continued on due south with his eyes fixed firmly on the far horizon.

For three days Thirsty Horse walked towards that horizon and saw nothing else, which did not surprise him since he expected to walk for two weeks before he would reach the border of the desert itself. Yet at around noon of the fourth day a rather strange thing happened. For it seemed to him that from time to time he could make out a strange sight in the far, far distance. It seemed incredible; but if he were not mistaken he was walking towards a ger camp of men - and one of very great size indeed!

Now Thirsty Horse knew perfectly well that he had not gone nearly far enough to reach even the border of the true desert, let alone to be able to see all the way to its far side. So what would a settlement of such a size as that be doing out here so far from the good grass lands to the north and elsewhere? Indeed, it was a situation that defied all possible reason - unless, perhaps, it was a mirage such as he had learned of in school? He resolved his surprise by concluding finally that that was what it must be. Yet as he came closer the mirage did not behave as his education had taught him that it should. For it neither shimmered in the light nor disappeared, but only grew bigger and firmer in his vision. Until eventually he was forced to think that perhaps it was real – and that he should be surprised after all!

It took Thirsty Horse another four hours of walking from when he caught his first half believed glimpse of that improbable sight until he came close enough to see it for what it really was. But then he saw, spread out before him, nothing more nor less than the great ger camp of men that he had first thought it to be. A ger camp of such vast extent, what's more, as to be a city beyond his wildest imaginings and no less than the full promise of his mirage confirmed as a shocking reality before him. While still he wondered what on earth such a settlement was doing out here, so isolated and hidden from any eyes save his own.

Now it was precisely because this find was so strange that it left one thought very clear in his mind: that his destiny had led him here as surely as the sun rose in the sky each morning, and all that remained for him to do now was to find out why. So on he walked towards the camp, a little daunted by the size of the city he approached. Fearing in consequence for what he would find, but never doubting, all the same - that find it he must.

...

Thirsty Horse had walked into many settlements of men in the past four years since his journey had begun and he had always found their peoples to be welcoming and friendly. Indeed, since he himself carried no apparent threat nor any evidence of wealth, then why should they not? Seeing no reason why his experience should be any different this time, he entered the great camp expecting neither more nor less from its people than this same familiar reception.

When he crossed the frontier of the city he found a bustle of movement and an energy that was surely beyond the normal activity of people and that pleased him, although he wondered why it should be. He saw many armed men on horseback too, all charging about the camp at great speed as if they had somewhere to go. But strangely not seeming, he thought to himself after he had watched them for a while, to be going anywhere in particular after all.

As for the welcome he received, though, the people of the great camp did not deign to treat him with such friendly familiarity as he was used to, and in fact it would have been truer to say that they completely ignored his presence altogether. Yet Thirsty Horse found no threat in this and considered it, in fact, to be no more than a trait of character occasioned by the magnificence of this city. Its citizens, at least for the moment, understandably too grand to stoop to the welcome of a poor and dusty traveller such as he. He did not notice that there were some there who looked at him suspiciously and then went very quickly upon their business - whatever that might be? And it did not occur to him that perhaps these same persons would have challenged him too, if only they had possessed the courage so to do!

Neither, of course, did he realise why they would need such courage, although in truth the reason was obvious enough. For here was Thirsty Horse, a boy of seventeen years old when he walked into the great camp: tall, well muscled and tough, and dressed in clothes that told of the harsh experiences of his journey. All he owned he carried upon his back together with enough water to survive a desert, and a big heavy stick that was all he needed should he meet by chance with a robber, or a rabid dog, or even a hungry mountain leopard. While everything about him, from his dusty boots and faded clothes to the straightness of his back and the look upon his face, spoke of independence and of pride. So all who saw him knew that here indeed was a young man as tough as the mountains had made him by their crossing; and just as he had looked to be the strongest horse in the

herd, so he looked the part he took now. Since, too, he was a stranger here and no one knew if his measure matched his looks or not, it really was quite simply the case that not one of those who cared to challenge him - would dare!

But still there were facts to be faced and dealt with, as Thirsty Horse knew well enough. He could not acceptably sleep out upon the streets of this settlement nor even stay here very long without making contact with its people. For such behaviour is not the way of man when he settles in one place. Since it seemed that no one would ever talk to him, however, he finally decided that there was only one possible thing to do. So finding a spot that was suitable in that it was much frequented by passers by, yet not blocking anyone's way, Thirsty Horse sat down and took from his back his guitar. He tuned it very carefully to make sure that the music would sound as sweet as it should, and then he began to play.

Now as Thirsty Horse played a crowd began to gather and listen, which finally was something that did not surprise him for that was as it should be. Yet there was something about the crowd that he could not understand. Because in how they stared at him now, and how they listened to him play, it seemed to Thirsty Horse that no one of his audience had ever heard music before! So the crowd listened in silence as he played, and when he stopped playing they did not applaud but simply waited patiently until he started to play again - while no one ever said a word.

For quite some time Thirsty Horse continued to play to his strangely silent audience and never received even so much as a murmur of approval for his playing. Yet still he received a very distinct impression that they did appreciate his music, and indeed that the hearts and minds of his silent audience were not so far beyond his reach as they appeared - and that was a situation to be explored. So after he had played a few calming and lyrical melodies and he felt that he had the attention of his audience sufficiently, Thirsty Horse chose a different kind of song – and he began to sing. And since the song seemed right for the moment it was a song of courage and of beauty that he sang. It seemed, too, that he had been right to choose this song, for very soon there was a murmur of response that went up through the crowd while he sang. Then as soon as the murmur began it was followed by a voice, which was exactly what Thirsty Horse had hoped for - except that the voice came not rising to the spirit of the song, but rather to crush it before it could rise too high!

"Hey you!" the voice called out roughly from before him. "Who are you and what are you doing here?" - which caused Thirsty Horse to stop his playing.

In truth, Thirsty Horse did not much like the tone of this voice; and when he looked up and saw its owner: a big powerful man with a sword in his hand and the sneer of a bully upon his face, did not like him any more than his voice. Yet he kept his own voice calm and polite while he replied, for he realised that he did not know this situation nor what it could become.

"As for my name," he said, "my name is Thirsty Horse. As for what I am doing here, I am a traveller passing through."

"Indeed." snorted the bully. "If you are a traveller, then from where have you come to arrive here?"

"Form the north across the mountains I have come." Thirsty Horse explained, and he kept his voice still very calm and polite. "But please tell me for I do not know - where is here?"

"Where is here?" the bully repeated loudly. "Hah! If really you do not know, then it is better that you do not learn either.

"But I don't trust you, though!" continued the bully. "I think you know very well that here is the great camp of the Great Han Khan the Magnificent, Lord of the Eternal Horde, King of all the Mongols and Emperor of all the World."

"Indeed!" said Thirsty Horse, understandably impressed and really quite excited too by this news. For surely this was an introduction to someone who would know the answer to his question: someone who would know the secret of life?

"Indeed." sneered the bully in reply. "And now you had better come with me. You've already caused enough trouble here."

"Indeed?" said Thirsty Horse, rather amazed to hear this, and he looked the bully in the eye to see if the man would give an explanation, but the bully said nothing more. Since he did not, Thirsty Horse then looked around for the faces of his audience to see if, perhaps, he could read an answer there. But there was no answer to be found there, simply because every member of his audience had quietly disappeared.

"Indeed." thought Thirsty Horse silently to himself; and he wondered what strange portent, indeed, was held within this scene.

But whatever the portents may have been, there was nothing for it now but to obey this bully's command. So Thirsty Horse followed him where he led for quite some time until they approached what must be the centre of the city, for the gers were now packed unusually close together. Then suddenly they came into a clearing where there stood a single ger that was much bigger than the others and very royally painted too.

"Now this," thought Thirsty Horse to himself, "must be the ger of the Great Han Khan the Magnificent, Lord of the Eternal Horde, King of all the Mongols and Emperor of all the World" - and of course he was right.

…

Before the great ger there stood two huge men at guard and the bully now whispered to one of these guards his explanation, presumably, for his visit now.

"Wait here," commanded the guard considerably more loudly, "and I will announce your presence to the Great Han Khan."

So Thirsty Horse and the bully waited patiently until the guard returned and reported rather pompously, "The Great Han Khan the Magnificent, Lord of the Eternal Horde, King of all the Mongols and Emperor of all the World, has agreed to hear you. Take your prisoner inside and explain yourself."

"So!" thought Thirsty Horse to himself. "Now I am a prisoner! And is it not a sad state indeed when the hospitality of a people to a visiting stranger amounts to no more than that?" But he kept his tongue and said nothing at this time, judging it better to wait until he had spoken with the Great Han Khan himself. While the thought also crossed his mind that perhaps then he would find, after all, that there was some good reason for all of this mistrust.

When Thirsty Horse first saw the inside of the Great Ger he could not help himself from gasping aloud at the splendour of what he saw, for splendour indeed is what it was. The walls were draped all around with the most beautiful and incredible cloth. Rich and heavy and of a quality beyond dispute, it was dyed with a purple dye to a dark depth that was an evocation of wealth and power. Yet as if that were not enough the cloth was threaded through with a shameless opulence of gold. Surely this would have been the most beautiful cloth that

Thirsty Horse had ever seen, or could ever even have dreamt of, in all his life. Except that in the centre of the ger there was draped another array of cloth - and that was the most beautiful cloth that this world has ever seen! For that cloth was woven from a thread of pure gold that shimmered under the lights within the ger, while scenes of mystery were subtly depicted within its depths by no more than the technique of its weaving. This cloth was of a beauty beyond that of any other upon this earth, and of that there could be no question at all. Inside the draping of gold cloth there was a throne, and upon the throne there sat a huge and very powerfully built man dressed in clothes appropriate to his setting - obviously the Great Han Khan himself.

Not one of the guards dared to speak before the Great Han Khan; while as for Thirsty Horse, whether he would dare to or not, he chose not to. For he judged, and correctly of course, that this was the wisest course of action that he could take.

The Great Han Khan looked at Thirsty Horse for quite some time in uninterrupted silence, until he was satisfied that he had learned as much as he could, or he wanted to, from what he saw, and then he spoke,

"Guardsman, present your prisoner and tell me what you know of him."

"Oh Great Han Khan the Magnificent, Lord of the Eternal Horde, King of all the Mongols and Emperor of all the World." the bully commenced. " He is a spy and a trouble maker and I have evidence of that. For I caught him in the act of trying to provoke public discontent by the playing of music in the streets, in disregard of our great and just law which wisely forbids such shameful perversions. I stopped him and questioned him, whereupon he continued his shameless contempt by lying to me: saying that he is just a visitor passing through. Other than that I know no more of him than that he claims his name to be Thirsty Horse, which seems very unlikely, and so I humbly submit that in this I do not believe him either."

The Great Han Khan had listened attentively to all that the guardsman said, and when he had finished he thought about it for a while before he pronounced dissmissively, "Thank you, guardsman. You have done well." Then he turned to address Thirsty Horse.

"So, prisoner." began the Great Han Khan. "You claim to be no more than an innocent stranger passing through and that your name is Thirsty Horse. While my guardsman chooses to believe that you are instead a spy, a troublemaker and a liar - and I, for myself, tend to agree with him, since even the very look of you gives truth to this summation.

"Such as you we do not want here and I think that for the good of all it is best to put you quickly to death." continued the Great Khan" - and mercifully so before the account of your crimes necessitates a more demonstrative execution." he finished.

Now these words came as a most unpleasant shock to Thirsty Horse, to say the least! But whatever the shock, he stayed calm; and although he did not know it, it was wise that he did. For the Great Han Khan was testing him and despite his pronouncements had not as yet decided what to do with his prisoner other than to frighten him and thereby find out what he knew and what he was worth.

"However." continued the Great Khan, "I am a wise and just ruler, and powerful enough to indulge my sentimentality, which sometimes I do. So I will give you the chance to speak for yourself - and if your story pleases me, then perhaps it will save your life. But we shall see."

163

Then the Great Han Khan nodded briefly towards Thirsty Horse and said, "Please begin."

So Thirsty Horse told that he was a simple traveller who searched for the secret of life, since this task had been set for him by his teacher. But as for the Cup of Curiosity and his life as a horse before he became a boy, of that he did not tell. For in his heart he knew that there was no trust within this company; and it seemed to him, therefore, that he would do better to keep his secrets to himself. Indeed it seemed highly probable that he would have need of them later - and the element of surprise, too, in their use.

"And have you found the secret of life?" asked the Great Han Khan when Thirsty Horse had finished his tale.

"No." replied Thirsty Horse. "As yet I have not."

"Then I will tell you." replied the Great Khan. "The secret of life is simply this, that strength is all that matters. For victory is given always to the strongest and since it is he who keeps the record of all that passes, his word is always the truth, whatever it may be.

"So tell me now before I decide your fate." he continued. "What strength have you, Thirsty Horse – if, indeed, that is your name - that you may lend to my assistance if I spare your life?"

"That is easy." replied Thirsty Horse, who after all his schooling had no fear of a question such as this. "I have great strength of body that is closer to a horse than to a man. While as for my mind, I have a good education from which I have learned of this world; and I have learned, too, the process of logical thought and can avoid the distractions of foolish illusion in my analysis. As for my heart, that I can express in the language of music and so move the hearts of others to better things, or worse, if I so wish. Beyond that, of course, I have

165

travelled over most of this land and know it well from north to south, and from one end to the other."

"Really." said the Great Khan thoughtfully. "Then I hold, Thirsty Horse, that you are a dangerous boy indeed!'"

To which Thirsty Horse, who was beginning to get the measure of his interlocutor by now, replied, "Yes, Oh Great Han Khan the Magnificent, Lord of the Eternal Horde, King of all the Mongols and Emperor of all the World. You are very wise and deduce correctly that it could be so. Yet you have nothing to fear from me, Oh Great Han Khan, for I come in peace as a simple traveller in search of nothing more than the answer to my question as set to me by my teacher."

To which the Great Khan responded immediately in turn, "But now I have answered your question for you, Thirsty Horse, and so you have no further need to travel. Surely then you will join me, should I offer you a place within my realm. Or do you not accept my answer and stand, therefore, in contempt of my wisdom and my word?"

Now this was a difficult moment for Thirsty Horse and he did not easily decide upon what he said next. Yet finally he replied, and with as much courage and diplomacy as he could balance together, "Oh Great Han Khan the Magnificent, Lord of the Eternal Horde, King of all the Mongols and Emperor of all the World. Your answer is most wise and I do not doubt that it is correct. Yet if I am to understand it and all the implications that it holds for all of mankind, then I must think upon it for a while at least so that the full extent of its wisdom may become clear to me. Only then, Oh Great Han Khan, will I be able to understand your answer in all the complication of its aspects, as I have been trained by my education to do."

Now when he heard this answer from Thirsty Horse, a look of the most terrible anger flashed upon the face of the Great Han Khan - yet there was another thought that occurred to him too at the same moment. For here was a boy who had travelled across all the land of Mongolia, further even and by far than the Great Khan himself had ever travelled. A boy, too, who had the education, or so he claimed, to understand what he had seen during his travels. Such were the facts and before them even the Great Han Khan, who certainly did not lack for intelligence himself, had to accept that here, indeed, was a boy who could yet prove to be of value. Not only that, but it was even possible that this boy was a gift from the powers of destiny - and as such, a gift that came with a trick of destiny too! For would the Great Han Khan recognise this gift and gain from it, or would he act rashly upon his pride and thereby lose it? It was exactly the kind of decision upon which history has been known to turn. So the Great Khan decided, finally, that he would accept this gift from destiny but that he would test it too - and as his first test he would offer Thirsty Horse a way out of his dilemma by the medium of a single question that he would ask him now. Yet the Great Khan also decided, at that same moment, that if Thirsty Horse failed in any of these tests he should be killed that very day – if he did not die by the test itself that is! For if he really were a gift from destiny, then surely he would have the intelligence to save himself from this fate?

"Tell me, Thirsty Horse." asked the Great Han Khan. "If you do not accept my answer now, then do you have another, or better, to consider in its place?"

"Oh Great Han Khan the Magnificent, Lord of the Eternal Horde, King of all the Mongols and Emperor of all the World." replied Thirsty Horse without hesitation. "Most certainly I do not." For Thirsty Horse had understood the test.

"Very well then." said the Great Han Khan by way of a prelude to his pronouncement on the matter of Thirsty Horse's immediate future. "I give you leave to stay as a guest within my realm for as long as it may please me for you to stay, and by this grace you may decide for yourself the course of your destiny – if you are quick enough to make your decision before the end of my patience is reached, that is. If you are, then we shall see which wisdom you believe, Thirsty Horse; and we shall see too, of course, if you have really the courage to follow it wherever it leads."

So the Great Han Khan the Magnificent, Lord of the Eternal Horde, King of all the Mongols and Emperor of all the World, had made his pronouncement and Thirsty Horse awaited no more than to be dismissed. Yet to his surprise the Great Han Khan did not dismiss him, but instead changed his voice to a much softer tone and invited, "But before you go to contemplate this great wisdom, Thirsty Horse, rest with me here a while and we shall talk together, you and I alone."

Then with a careless wave of his hand, the Great Han Khan dismissed his guards, who all bowed very low and left, walking backwards as they went so as not to turn their backs upon their king, and without saying a word.

...

Once they were alone the Great Khan summoned Thirsty Horse, in a much softer voice, to come closer to his throne, and then to sit down upon a large cushion that was placed before it. And the significance of this honour was not lost on Thirsty Horse as he sank into the luxurious comfort of the cushion and realised that this was a privilege granted to very few.

When the Great Han Khan began to speak he continued in that same softer tone of his voice that he had used for the first time just a moment ago; and as Thirsty Horse listened, he realised why. For he understood that the Great Han Khan, for all his power and all his majesty, really had not seen so much of the world as he would have his subjects believe. Not really enough, even, to know if his plans to conquer it were founded upon the stuff of reality, or would simply flounder as foolish dreams. In fact the Great Han Khan, to put it another way, had sometimes still to keep the yapping dogs of his doubt at bay. While as for Thirsty Horse, when he realised this truth, he knew for certain that neither did the Great Han Khan know the answer to his question, "What is the secret of life?"

"The history of my clan," began the Great Han Khan, "has been one of hardship: of enemies, of wars, and of troubles. So much so, in fact, that when I was born my people were scattered wide upon this land and no one of us was living any better than the weather and his fortunes allowed. In such small groups, what's more, that it was easy for our enemies to mount raiding parties against us and we were ever a prey to those raids. That was how it was when I was a boy, and by the time I became a man, Thirsty Horse – nothing had changed at all.

"But it was not in my heart to see my people preyed upon at will by our enemies and so it was I, alone from us all, who stood forth for war against our foes and for freedom from our oppression. It was I alone who rode forth upon my horse with my head held high and my sword raised to rally the clans to war.

"How rude was my disappointment, though, at how my people responded to my call. For there were some who laughed, and many who simply turned away, but very few indeed who would listen to me; and none, finally, who rode to follow me. But then, I thought, it must be that I have first to earn their respect before they will trust their fortunes to me. For how could they know that I would not just turn and run away as soon as our enemies fired the first bullet or arrow back?

"Once I realised this I knew what I had to do to win their respect and I set out to do it that very night, at the expense of one particular band of robbers who had just launched an attack from close by. Since these robbers had encountered very little resistance it seemed to me that they would be complacent in their victory. So I set out to find their camp, which I did without too much trouble, then I hid myself at some small distance away to watch and to wait. When night fell I observed their celebrations and waited still; and once they had finished and slept - still I waited. Finally I waited until two hours had passed since they had fallen asleep, but no more, then I crept slowly forward towards their camp, and quietly so as not to alert their guards.

"Now is it any surprise to you, Thirsty Horse, after all that I have said, that they had only set one guard, or that I found him to be drunk and asleep? But surprise or not, it was good fortune indeed for me – for I took my knife and turned his sleep into death without so much as a sound. After that the task that I had imagined to be the most dangerous challenge of my life proved to be nothing much at all, as quickly I moved from sleeping man to sleeping man and liberated each one from the hardships of this world. Their leader I found last and when I had killed him, I cut off his head to take back with me as evidence of my victory.

"The next day when I rode out again amongst my people I held the head of our enemy before me – and then the people were afraid at the thought of the revenge that this act would surely bring upon them. And that, even though I told them that all of that particular band of robbers were dead.

"After a week had gone by, though, and no revenge had come, then my people realised that what I had said was true - yet still they did not follow me and I could not understand why? When another band of robbers attacked us a week after that, I decided that I had had enough. So I rode out again amongst my people and I picked out 2 young men as my soldiers. Then I told them simply that their choice was to follow me or to die there and then. I raised my sword high as I spoke - and they did not dare to refuse. So that, Thirsty Horse, was the beginning of my army.

"From that day on my power continued to grow. And now here I am the Great Han Khan: Lord of all this steppe, and my enemies all defeated."

Since the Great Khan had obviously finished his recital, Thirsty Horse now took his turn to speak, "Then you have performed a great service for your people, Oh Great Han Khan, and that is an admirable achievement indeed. You have no more enemies to defeat and your people may live, therefore, in freedom and in peace."

"Ah, but no." continued the Great Khan, "For as you who have travelled will surely know, times have changed from those simple days. It is not so far from here that our enemies gather in force to attack us once again - and would this very night, I do not doubt, if they but detected a weakness in our defences. Or you may tell me, Thirsty Horse, if you do not consider that this is so?"

Then Thirsty Horse thought for a moment, before he replied carefully, "As for your enemies, Oh Great Han Khan, I cannot say. For there are places yet that I have not seen and journeys that I have not made. Perhaps it is that they are camped to the east of here, where I have never been. But all I can say for sure is that in all the length and breath of Mongolia that I have travelled, I have never met their like. Then he ventured hesitantly, "And it seems to me, Oh Great Han Khan, that the tale you tell is a strange one indeed for this land today."

Now when Thirsty Horse spoke these words a rather strange thing happened. For the face of the Great Han Khan that within this hour of intimate revelation had held such a mild and pleasant expression, slowly contorted into a most horrible sneer! Then when he spoke again his voice had changed to take on such a low and sinister tone that Thirsty Horse imagined a snake in human form, "My people lived as slaves and would still if I had not freed them." said the Great Khan. "So what, then, should be the price of their freedom if it is not the service that they owe to me now. That service they may repay me by their lives in battle against my enemies, if that is called for. Or if it is not, then they may live to serve me in any way I choose. Because I am the strongest – and my will is the law. For them, and for all who come before me."

Seeing the face of the Great Han Khan so distorted and hearing these words so venomously hissed in these tones of hatred, a very strange thought came to Thirsty Horse. For he suddenly wondered if there was any truth at all in the story that the Great Han Khan had just told! Indeed, he thought, how could it possibly be true? Because in all his travels Thirsty Horse had never encountered anything, not any man nor any experience at all, that would give the least substance to this picture of a world of enemies and war that the Great Khan painted now! Certainly there were many examples of it in history, it was true. But here and now? It was contrary to everything that Thirsty Horse had seen in all his travels and it simply could not, therefore, be more improbable. But still, Thirsty Horse had not seen everything that the world had to offer as he had already and freely admitted. So perhaps the world did change its course over the next hill?

"Maybe – or maybe not." Thought Thirsty Horse. "Or maybe there is something wrong with the story that Han Khan tells of his world – and I must say that to me that seems more likely." But he said nothing of this, of course, for whatever was wrong with the story that the Great Han Khan had told, Thirsty Horse did not know enough to understand it yet. While he realised too that the present situation would be better served by wisdom and patience than by confrontation. So instead he replied very simply and clearly, and certainly with a little dishonesty too, although it went much against his usual principles,

"Yes, Oh Great Han Khan. You are right."

The Great Han Khan considered Thirsty Horse suspiciously for a moment, but then seemed satisfied with this response. So he continued,

"Here, Thirsty Horse, I have raised an army that is greater still than any army that this land has ever seen and with my army I will sweep across the steppe and conquer all in my path. That day will come for it is my destiny and I feel within my heart that it will be soon. When it does, Thirsty Horse, then there will be no corner of Mongolia, or indeed of all the world, that is not within my power.

"But it is easy to talk." continued the Great Khan. "Even to talk of armies that will conquer the world, and perhaps you do not believe me after all?"

To which Thirsty Horse replied quickly. "I assure you, Oh Great Han Khan, that I most certainly believe all that you say."

"Thirsty Horse." said the Great Khan then with almost a note of fond familiarity in his voice. "It is just as well that you do. But still I have prepared a demonstration so that you may see my power for yourself, just in case you did not. So come, my young guest, for the best of my army is assembled and waiting to show you their force at arms and their horsemanship. While for me such demonstration is one of the few true and simple pleasures that may be claimed by a king."

Then Thirsty Horse and the Great Han Khan left the Great Ger and were carried in ceremony for quite some way until they reached the open steppe at the edge of the town where the army of the Great Han Khan was assembled.

...

Never had Thirsty Horse ever seen, or even so much as dreamt in fact, of a gathering like this. There were rank upon rank of cavalry and all mounted upon the most magnificent and beautifully groomed horses. All fully armed and regally magnificent in costumes that combined both armour and art to make the most incredible display imaginable.

"One thousand horsemen – waiting at my command." said the Great Han Khan very slowly and proudly. "Now how could I ever wish for a greater sight than that? And yet even that, Thirsty Horse, even that is only the best of my army and by a very long count, certainly not all."

Then as Thirsty Horse watched, a single horse suddenly snorted and reared its head, which set a reaction of impatience to tremble through the ranks and make the presence of these one thousand horses and one thousand men become even more passionately alive. While in response to the impatience of his forces, the Great Han Khan stood up and raised his arms high to hold the attention of his commanders for a moment. Then suddenly he gave the grand gesture that they all awaited and the display began.

First a tremendous roar of human voices went up and all the horses reared at the same time, making the army look as if each man and horse stood as a centaur, 10 feet tall. Then the army organised very quickly to different formations of cavalry and the display of horsemanship began, just as the Great Khan had said it would.

As for Thirsty Horse, he was completely and utterly enraptured and enthralled by the magnificence of the spectacle. Such flashing colours, such speed and skill, and such a thunder of hooves as the army passed that they made the ground shake beneath his feet. It was truly so awesome a sight that its accomplishment by men made him proud to be one of their kind; while equally so its thunder of hooves made him proud to have once been a horse. So however this day had begun and whatever it might finally bring, this moment, at least, he would count amongst the best that he had ever known during all his life.

For perhaps an hour this display of charging cavalry, of archery on horseback, and of mock battle, continued; until it concluded when the army reformed their ranks and files before the Great Khan in the same manner as before. Then to a new formation the division commanders and their standard bearers all rode forward to give their salute, while before them the three generals of the army stood proud and gave their salute too. That was the moment when the Great Han Khan the Magnificent, Lord of the Eternal Horde, King of all the Mongols and Emperor of all the World, stood up before the best one thousand horsemen of his army and returned their salute. The moment when the hush of the spectacle suddenly exploded into the roar of the crowd; and that was the moment too when Thirsty Horse saw for the first time in his life what it means to be a king, and found himself to be awed at the sight.

Having given his salute, the Great Han Khan sat down again looking even more than usually pleased with himself. Then he turned to Thirsty Horse and said, "Here is my army, ready to conquer the world, and which I have graciously invited you to join. Although that, of course, is on the condition that you really do have some service of use to me - and at this very moment I rather doubt that you do. But perhaps," continued the Great Han Khan, "you would like this opportunity to prove to me your worth as a horseman and your fitness, thereby, to ride at my side. And for that, my young friend, I will send now for a horse for you to ride." After the magnificence of what had just passed, the Great Khan felt suddenly the desire to temper the mettle of his guest within the passions of the hour. While in this, also, was contained the second test!

Now Thirsty Horse was actually quite startled when he heard this invitation. He understood immediately that here was another test of the Great Han Khan and that it was again, most probably, a test that he must pass or forfeit his life! But as to whether he could pass it? Well, on the one hand he had never ridden a horse before in his life, while on the other hand he had once been a horse himself! So how would these two conflicting facts find him now as a horseman? In truth, Thirsty Horse suspected that he could ride, and probably quite well too, but he didn't know it for sure. While there was obviously no way to refuse the test - and that was his dilemma.

Yet whatever the outcome might eventually prove to be, Thirsty Horse stood up and bowed most graciously to the Great Han Khan; and then he said, speaking loudly so that as many as possible could hear him,

"Oh Great Han Khan the Magnificent, Lord of the Eternal Horde, King of all the Mongols and Emperor of all the World. It is my inestimable pleasure to accept the honour of your invitation." Then as he stood before the Great Han Khan, Thirsty Horse bowed very, very low indeed.

Thirsty Horse had decided to meet the challenge head on and with all the dignity that he could muster. Then if, as was certainly possible, he failed in this test. At least he would go out in style.

...

The stallion that they brought for Thirsty Horse to ride was truly a magnificent animal. Huge and powerful, he was easily the biggest horse that Thirsty Horse had ever seen. But he was, too, an animal so spirited that many horsemen thought him to be mad, while certainly no one had ever been able to ride him yet. Since this was the horse that they proposed for Thirsty Horse to ride, he wondered if they really expected that he could? Then suddenly it became very clear to him what the intention of the Great Han Khan really was. For such was the beauty and glory of the hour that what better way could there be to end it - than with a brave battle and a noble death! Yet whatever the harshness of this test that the Great Han Khan had designed for Thirsty Horse, it was not so harsh that it could not be countered by the workings of fortune. For such workings can sometimes be very strange indeed.

In truth Thirsty Horse did not fear the great stallion, since he had tricks up his sleeve to befriend a horse more than any man or boy who had ever lived. As for his own untried ability to ride a horse at all, though, that did continue to worry him. So it was good luck indeed, however strangely come by, that at that moment he heard the sound of unkind laughter come once again to his ears to remind him of his moments of past shame. For it was that, and nothing else, that made Thirsty Horse decide there and then that he would be the best horseman that the world had ever seen - and he set his heart to the task.

Then Thirsty Horse spoke to the great stallion in the language of the Horses, although it came strangely accented now from his boy's tongue. Yet the stallion understood him well enough, and after he had first reared in surprise, he listened to the words of this strange boy as he said, "Will you not consent to let me ride you this one time, friend. For you should know that we are cousins, you and I, even though my fortune has led me upon a stranger path than any other horse has ever taken. And you should know, too, that if we ride together now then it will be to change the very destiny itself - of this world at least."

So the great stallion agreed to let Thirsty Horse ride him, and Thirsty Horse rode harder and faster than any man in the army of the Great Han Khan had ever ridden before. So much so, in fact, that everyone who saw him ride remarked upon it. While as for those men who had sniggered behind his back when first Thirsty Horse had met the stallion, they had heard him speak in the language of the horses to tame the great beast. Certainly, too, they hastened to set rumour of that story upon the ears of all; and that was a rumour that would grow to be a legend before even the hour was out, or Thirsty Horse had finished his ride. As for the result of that rumour it was simply this, that every man within the army of the Great Han Khan began to wonder what greater glory might result from following Thirsty Horse, rather than their king!

As for the Great Han Khan himself, he was forced to realise that the more he tested Thirsty Horse, the more important his strange guest became, and the more seriously, therefore, he was forced to take him. Now he had shown himself to be a horseman of such ability that surely he could turn the tale of a battle just by his presence alone; and then for the first time it crossed the mind of even the Great Han Khan himself to wonder - if still he dared to ride into battle without Thirsty Horse by his side?

Yet the last word to be recorded here should be for Thirsty Horse. For if the Great Han Khan had only asked him again, at that moment of the exchange of salutes, whether he wished to join his army, Thirsty Horse would not have been able to reply with any other word than a most definite "Yes." While now that he had been tested and had passed his test, he had the measure of the Great Han Khan and his army and the moment of his awe before this new vision of power and might had passed. But then such is the working of fortune as all who are wise will know.

…

"You are indeed fortunate, Thirsty Horse," the Great Han Khan began his speech back in the Great Ger, "to arrive here at this time, so soon before the day when my power will reach out for its due conquest. For to you is given the chance to help me while still I may take some small benefit from your help. And now you have been even more fortunate, for you have seen something of my army too and so you know that my plan will soon become reality."

Then the Great Han Khan posed a question that he did not expect to be answered against him, for he asked, "Or you may tell me, if you believe that it is so, that destiny does not favour my plans? That at some point in all your travels, perhaps, you have seen another army that would make a match for mine?"

Having said this, the Great Khan paused to look at Thirsty Horse while he waited for his answer; and Thirsty Horse replied with honesty and no hesitation at all, "No, Oh Great Han Khan. I have never seen it's like, nor even so much as the shadow of its like." For that, indeed, was the simple truth.

"Now that is good." said the Great Han Khan, noting with a smile of satisfaction that Thirsty Horse had been truly sincere in his response. "Your words are all that I have been waiting so long to hear and now I am ready to ride with my army to the destruction of all who stand in my way. So join with me now, Thirsty Horse, while my invitation still holds its warmth. Then in recognition of your strength, your knowledge, and your horsemanship, which you will use to my benefit alone, I will make of you a commander of very high rank. Then you may profit greatly from your efforts and amass a wealth of gold and riches with your victories."

That is what the Great Han Khan said to Thirsty Horse. But what he thought to himself and did not say was this: that here was a boy who possessed the power to move men in their hearts, and even if today he did it with a song, tomorrow he would hold a sword in his hand -for it was clear that his destiny would call him to it. Now if such as he were not within the power of the Great Han Khan – then it was beyond any doubt that he would be far too dangerous a competitor to be left alive!

As for Thirsty Horse, however, it was rather the idea of wealth and riches that had caught his imagination at that moment – and that because it was difficult for him to understand the principle at all! His life's reward had always been to fulfil his dreams, and his dreams were to play music and to find the secret of life. What need, then, could he ever have for more than this: that his music was listened to; that his belly was sometimes full, but also sometimes empty so that he did not forget the pleasure of food; that he did not freeze to death in winter, and that he continued in his search for the answer to his question? What other profit, indeed, could there possibly be?

Nevertheless he replied courteously and wisely, "Please accept my apologies for my failing of this moment, Oh Great Khan, but I cannot accept your offer yet. For such is the honour that you do me and so generous beyond measure, that first I must give it the consideration and the gravity that it deserves." Then he added, because he had suddenly remembered something that his teacher had said, "Within my heart I know of only one place on earth where I will find such calm and silence as will permit the contemplation that is due to your offer. And I realise now, Oh Great Khan, that it is there I must go; and it is of the desert that I speak."

Now when the Great Han Kahn heard these words from Thirsty Horse yet another look of anger flashed across his face, for really his patience was being tested this day. Yet after the day's events he knew only too well the value of having Thirsty Horse at his side and no longer could he lightly take the chance of refusing this request. So Thirsty Horse was actually quite surprised, and more than a little grateful, when the Great Han Khan said dismissively, "Then go to the desert, Thirsty Horse, but do not be gone too long. For I await your answer with a patience that holds upon the reins of destiny – and I will not wait long."

. . .

Now all of this, although it is indeed so much to tell, is the story of just one day that Thirsty Horse passed within the camp of the Great Han Khan. It is a lot to tell because on that day Thirsty Horse was driven by the force of his destiny - and as Far Seeing Horse had said so long ago, "such days as those are very long indeed."

That night Thirsty Horse would have been grateful to fall at last into the sleep that his exhaustion deserved. Yet although he did sleep, and most comfortably too, still he did not sleep nearly so well or so deeply as he would have wished. For the thought that someone might cut his throat in the night had arisen very clearly in his mind.

. . .

The next day at dawn Thirsty Horse left for the desert as he had said he would – and he found that he was being followed! Now since he had never in his life been followed before he had to stop and think for a moment before he really knew what he thought about it. But then, when he had thought about it, he realised that the situation was not at all to his liking. For how would he ever be able to know the peace and the solitude of the desert in the knowledge that there were men

watching him from close by? So Thirsty Horse continued on walking until he passed for a moment behind a rock along the way. Then when he was out of sight he said the magic words and turned himself into a horse again. He was grateful that on this occasion the transformation was accomplished without the accompanying clap of thunder, although exactly how this was achieved he had no idea since it was part of the magic and therefore beyond him to know. Once he was a horse again, he galloped off alone and very quickly left his unwelcome followers far behind.

As for the two soldiers who had been following him, they returned with misery and shame in their hearts to explain their failure to the Great Han Khan. "It was only for a few seconds that Thirsty Horse disappeared behind the rock," they told, "yet we never saw him again! Only a horse galloping fast in the distance did we see - and that horse had no rider, not even one crouching low and to the horse's side. So where he went we do not know."

"Hmm!" said the Great Han Khan thoughtfully; and so deep was he then in his thoughts that he forgot immediately about these two soldiers save to give the briefest wave of his hand and dismiss them; while very gratefully they left. Once they were gone he continued for quite some time to contemplate deeply upon the report that he had just received, until finally he arrived at this summation that he voiced aloud, "These men are neither fools nor accustomed to failure, and from what they tell me I can only conclude that there is some unseen magic at work here. Some strange mechanism that is beyond their understanding and mine too, it seems - and yet, I believe, not beyond my strength. For Thirsty Horse does not dare to stand against me, not yet at least, and whether he runs now in fear or goes simply to consider my offer, as he says, is not clear. Yet one thing is clear to me now and that beyond any question at all. If Thirsty Horse does dare to come back here - then it will be to play this game in earnest, and to the death."

...

So the Great Han Khan talked to his guards and pondered thoughts of Destiny, yet no counterpart of his concerns came then to worry the mind of Thirsty Horse. For Thirsty Horse was a horse once again in that hour and he felt within his body a power that could run so far as to reach the edge of the steppe; and so fast as to leave even the wolves behind. While even that power had grown to a greater strength than ever before with his extra years and the endurance of the mountains now within his blood. Greater, too, was the simple delight in running that came again to his heart; and the consequence of that was that he ran, and ran, and ran, and ran - for nothing more than the joy of running upon the open steppe that he had missed so much. In fact so great was the joy of Thirsty Horse to run like this again, they say, that for the very first time since he had left the herd he began to wonder if all the world of men was really worth the loss of just this simple pleasure.

It is said, too, that it was because he could not answer this question that Thirsty Horse ran on, and on, and on - so far and so fast as he did. But whatever his motivation, such was the spirit within the heart of Thirsty Horse as he ran that day, that no other horse before or since has ever matched his pace. Some even say as well that so fast did his hoof beats fall and so strong did his heart beat to their rhythm, that for a while as he ran, time itself laid down its baton and took its measure from the beat of his hooves. Now I do not know, myself, if that is true. But it is a story that the horses tell and its truth lies with them; which is somewhere beyond the knowledge of men.

As for the wolves upon the desert that saw him pass, they did not even stir to give chase. For they knew immediately that it was far beyond their speed to ever catch a horse that ran so fast as this. It is even said, by the horses that is, that the wolves contented themselves to await the messengers of their own destiny for news of this ride of Thirsty Horse, and that they did not doubt that a messenger would come. Again I do not know myself, but it would not surprise me if the horses are right. For it is of these things and their like that the horses know well and I could not say either, that they are wrong.

But whatever the truth of these mysteries, all I know for sure is that Thirsty Horse ran so fast that day that he very quickly reached the end of the desertic steppe. That after that he crossed into the desert true and that still he did not stop running until he was half way across the desert itself – and that is a very long way indeed.

There did, of course, come a moment eventually when Thirsty Horse stopped. When by whatever magic of the desert that spoke to his soul, he knew quite suddenly that he had arrived at wherever he should be. So he stopped, and stood looking around at the landscape before him, while he breathed heavily to replenish the oxygen in his blood after all that running, and the sound of his breathing came terribly loud to his ears because from the desert itself there came no sound at all. So loud did Thirsty Horse's breathing sound in the desert silence, in fact, that it was not until he had fully recovered from his exertions; until his breathing and his heart had calmed completely, that he actually discovered the desert's silence for himself. And if you believe this story as the horses tell it, then you will believe too that it was at exactly that moment, when Thirsty Horse first heard the silence of the desert and nothing else at all, that time took up its baton and began again.

Now it was also in that moment that Thirsty Horse made a decision that he had been destined all along to make - and he made it well. For such is the power of the desert that even in those very first moments of his arrival it had already taught him where his heart lay.

"Horse, be a boy again." said Thirsty Horse, and he reared up upon his hind legs and gave out a great neighing as the thunder clap sounded in the sky above him, and of course he became a boy again. Then he sat down upon a rock with his chin resting upon his hands and there he remained for a long time, just as quiet and calm as the silence all around allowed him to be. There he gathered his thoughts together and he wondered about his quest, about himself, and about what to do next - and eventually the desert brought the answers to his mind. To be clear, he could not say that the desert actually spoke to him, since there was no ethereal voice that came to him from behind a rock nor any such magic as that. Yet the fact remains that it was in the silence of the desert that the answers came to Thirsty Horse and that was just as his teacher had said it would be.

The first thoughts that came to him were of the Great Han Khan. For here was a man who at this moment held the destiny of his world within his hands – and who was Thirsty Horse to say whether he held it well or crushed it without care? Who indeed? Yet the moment had come when Thirsty Horse must face this very question; and by the light of all that he had learned, decide himself between what was right and what was wrong - and why. Then most difficult of all, find the courage to believe in his decision - even if by believing he would then be forced to stand alone against all the world!

For destiny is not chance, Thirsty Horse believed, and it had not led him to this moment in his life just so that he could nod his head wisely and go cautiously on his way. So with the words of the Great Han Khan sounding still clear in his mind, Thirsty Horse set himself to pit all the learning and all the experience of his life to his consideration of those words.

"The secret of life," the Great Han Khan had said, "is simply this: that strength is all that matters. For victory is given always to the strongest and since it is he who keeps the record of all that passes, his word is always the truth, whatever it may be."

"Yet in his heart each man will always know the truth." Thirsty Horse remembered these words of the soldier in the mountains. While the words that had come to him then seemed to fit just as well in response to this question now, so he repeated them aloud. "No, they are wrong - those who do not listen to their hearts. For beneath the stars that shine above steppe and mountain alike; that grant to men the gifts they use to make their lives and their world; that set the truth and judge it in us all – they are wrong."

"How rude was my disappointment," the Great Han Khan had said too, "at how my people responded to my call. For there were some who laughed, and many who simply turned away, but very few indeed who would listen to me; and none, finally, who rode to follow me."

Thirsty Horse thought about this for a while too. But this time, as he pondered these words, he understood a very different interpretation to their significance. Was it not, perhaps, simply because there had been no war to fight other than in the mind of the Great Han Khan himself that no one had listened to him? Was it not, in fact, that all this tale of enemies was no more than a ruse that he had used to assume the power and position of a great military leader? While in reality there was no need for such in this day and age. Or if he truly believed in what he said, then was it not, finally, that there was nothing in all his talk of war and conquest – except for his own delusions?

Then suddenly Thirsty Horse realised beyond any doubt that the truth of the Great Han Khan's past was, of course, exactly as he now imagined it to be – nothing but his own delusions.

The Thirsty Horse of Mongolia

"Alas for the Great Han Khan," thought Thirsty Horse. "For here is a man who possesses such great and undoubted talents that he could have achieved so much to the good and benefit of all, if only something of his destiny had been different.

"In another time, indeed, his people would have been glad of him. Yet today he serves no other purpose than to dispense his tyranny for his own profit. Aye, for his own profit." Thirsty Horse repeated the words thoughtfully, and he realised exactly what the error of the Great Han Khan had been. "For profit," he said aloud once more, "and the word is well applied indeed. For it is clear to me now that the Great Han Khan has chosen to give his labour only for his own gain, and never has he cast so much as a single thought to the benefit or the suffering of any but himself."

Then suddenly it all became so very clear to Thirsty Horse that he pronounced aloud the revelation that the desert had brought him - so that even the rocks could hear, "Yet destiny demands of each man, for its fulfilment, that sometimes he will give of himself freely, then wait with patience to see what reward may come. For it is by that chance invited that destiny reveals the path for him to follow; and if a man does not make that sacrifice, then the true course of his destiny he will never find. So alas, indeed, for the Great Han Khan, whose mistake has been to replace his destiny with his ambition. For his ambition has led him to no more than a hollow illusion of grandeur that stands upon no foundation at all."

After that Thirsty Horse thought no more about the Great Han Khan, but concentrated his mind instead upon thoughts of the people who lived beneath his rule. When eventually he finished these contemplations too, it was with a very heavy heart that he reached his conclusion. For he knew now the course that he had to follow, and he knew that it would be a hard road indeed; and finally it was with this thought in mind that Thirsty Horse set out once more to return to the camp of the Great Han Khan.

Now it is customary to remember at this point in the tale, that strong as he was as a boy it took Thirsty Horse nearly four weeks to walk back the distance of that one day's ride that he had made as a horse. It is customary to remember, because it is a measure of how great the effort was that Thirsty Horse made on that journey to repay his debts for all that he had learned. His debts, as he understood them, to his teachers, certainly. But his debts, as well, to mankind, to the Great Earth Beneath the Stars and the Stars themselves, and to his destiny. While it is usually noted too that he nearly died of thirst on the journey, for there was precious little water along the way. Yet for all its hardships, Thirsty Horse did make that journey - and that is what is remembered most of all.

...

In the time from when he left until he walked back into the Great Camp, the people of the Great Han Khan had not forgotten Thirsty Horse. They had not forgotten him - but they had despaired of him!

So it was that when he was first sighted, walking slowly and determinedly towards the camp from the distant horizon, a murmur of fortune to come began to buzz excitedly within the population and people began to wonder what change to their destiny this fortune would bring. While perhaps they wondered too, for themselves, if they would have the courage and the conviction to rise up and match its mettle?

When Thirsty Horse reached the edge of the Great Camp he found in his heart that he wanted to sing, and so he did. As he walked onwards towards the Great Ger in the centre of the camp his singing grew louder and louder; and it was the same song of courage he sang, that he had sung on that very first day when he had arrived. This time, though, and far from the silence that had greeted him before, children ran out from their homes and began to follow him as he sang. Then other people followed him too, until by the time that Thirsty Horse arrived at the Great Ger there was such a following of people behind him that he had no need at all to announce his presence – not even to the Great Han Khan himself.

So the Great Han Khan had no choice, in fact, but to come out of his ger, accompanied by his guards of course, and to confront Thirsty Horse before his people where all could witness what was said - aye, and judge it for themselves!

The scene depicted by the protagonists was of two great and opposing forces of will standing each firm upon his ground and facing the other down. One the master of tyranny with an army at his command; while the other stood alone with no more for his protection than himself, and his trust in this destiny that he had not refused.

Fittingly, it was Thirsty Horse who spoke first, and it was most respectfully that he spoke too; for he began like this, "Oh Great Han Khan the Magnificent, Lord of the Eternal Horde, King of all the Mongols and Emperor of all the World, I offer you my greetings. I have travelled much since last we spoke, and I humbly offer you too the benefit of my thoughts and my experiences from the desert and my travels therein. This offer I am most happy to make, Oh Great Han Khan, for you have been most gracious in your generosity to me.

"I make my offer and I beg for your indulgence too. For my gifts are but the sum of myself and have no value that can be measured in gold. Yet I beg you sincerely, Oh Great Han Khan, for what I offer to you is the most valuable possession that I have to give."

Now it is said that when he heard this speech from Thirsty Horse, the Great Han Khan was seen to hesitate for a moment. In fact it is even said by some that he appeared to be seriously considering the offer that Thirsty Horse had made. But then, it is noted too, he seemed to suddenly reach his decision – and the moment of his hesitation was gone forever, as he replied, "This is all very well, Thirsty Horse, yet it seems to me that you forget who you are. For do you not recognise that you are nothing but a boy of no consequence at all? And how can it be that such as you may grant to himself the right to speak his mind before me? So spare me please your pointless platitudes and your foolish arrogance and concern yourself only with the one issue that matters here. I know that you remember very well, Thirsty Horse, that I made you an offer before you left, and I consider myself unusually generous to you in that my offer still stands. But now I would like to hear that you accept it - before I change my mind as I am more than sorely tempted to do."

Then the Great Han Khan completed his summary in a voice become suddenly more sinister than ever it had been before, "Or do you dare to come back here, Thirsty Horse, armed with nothing more than your arrogance, and considering that your right to defy a king?

Before the menace of this final ultimatum, Thirsty Horse said nothing for a few seconds, while everyone there stood silent and looked towards him. Then he bowed very low indeed before the Great Han Khan and he held his bow for a long time too. But when he straightened himself up again he stood very tall and straight before the king, and he said in a voice that rang as clearly as any bell could sound,

"Oh Great Han Khan the Magnificent, Lord of the Eternal Horde, King of all the Mongols and Emperor of all the World, my answer to you - is no."

And the word resounded between the Great Han Khan and Thirsty Horse like the cry of a lost soul echoing within the silence of doom.

But not for long did it echo before the Great Han Khan's face soured to a look of the purest hatred possible. Then he raised his head and his voice and he proclaimed to all,

"So, my people, here is Thirsty Horse. A boy who has come before you by your good fortune, although not by his, to show you so that you may know, the penalty for defiance of your king." Then the Great Han Khan lowered his voice again to its most sinister and said,

"Guards! Take this boy now and beat him to death upon the ground where he stands. Then cut off his head and set it upon a spear in this place so that all may know the destiny that follows after any such impudent fool as he!"

So the guards grabbed hold of Thirsty Horse to mete out this punishment, while even as they did an angry growl of disapproval went up from the crowd! For in that moment the hearts of Han Khan's people were not with their king, but sided with Thirsty Horse. In fact, such was the feeling of the crowd at that moment that it could easily have seen the end of the Great Han Khan then and there.

It didn't, however, and that it didn't was because the Great Khan knew only too well that he held his rule by might alone; and why, therefore, should he have trusted to the fondness of his people now when never he had before? So it was by careful design that 100 horsemen, all hand picked for their loyalty and highly paid for this very moment, rode suddenly forward to block the crowd from saving Thirsty Horse. Still it is said that the crowd could have held sway over the horsemen, for indeed they were many. Thus it is said too that what won the moment for the Great Han Khan, finally, was that in their hearts his people did not find the courage to stand fast to their conviction - but hesitated to their loss.

With no one now to stand by his side, Thirsty Horse found himself alone and helpless in the power of the Great Khan's guardsmen - and they showed him no mercy at all! They pushed him quickly to the ground and began to kick and beat him as they had been commanded to do - while all the crowd that had followed him looked on aghast. They smashed his guitar, of course, and they would have killed him quickly. For it was clearly wise to dispense with such a threat as he without delay.

Yet they did not kill Thirsty Horse, for as the story is told, and I of course know it to be true, it was at that very moment that he cried aloud the magic words,

"Boy, be a horse again!"

Suddenly the sky became almost black and there was an enormous clap of thunder, louder than anyone had ever heard before. So loud, in fact, that even the guardsmen leapt back in amazement at the sudden shock of the noise. Then as they watched - the transformation took place! Thirsty Horse regained the body of a horse that could run faster than time: and no four guardsmen on earth, nor even any army complete, could ever have held back that spirit.

Then Thirsty Horse reared up as tall as any horse has ever stood, kicking with his fore hooves into the air and neighing with all the power that his great lungs could muster. While all those who watched, people, guards, soldiers and horsemen, and even the Great Han Khan himself, were shocked to fear and amazement by this magic that had taken place before them.

The Thirsty Horse of Mongolia

So Thirsty Horse was free! But rather than run away and make good his escape as he could have done, he reared again and jumped onto a cart nearby. Then once more he spoke the magic words to produce yet another awesome clap of thunder from the heavens; and to become again – a boy.

Of course everyone there just stared in silence at Thirsty Horse. For no one had ever seen a boy become a horse before, let alone turn back into a boy afterwards; and they feared to know what would happen next. While it is said, and it is certainly true, that in that moment Thirsty Horse held such power to inspire the hearts of the crowd that he could have changed their world to be whatever he wished – and indeed, that is what he intended to do.

The speech that Thirsty Horse made then is often told just for its own sake; and it is thought by most to have been a very good speech. Although there are some who hold it in far higher esteem than that, and I would count myself as one of them. This is the speech that he gave,

"Imagination to be inspired; ingenuity to achieve and enough strength to achieve it with; courage to dare; memory to build upon; intelligence to bind it all into one; and compassion for all the world. These are the gifts of the Stars to men and they pass to us all for a moment; so that each and every one of us may have the chance to use them to the best accomplishment that he can: by that to realise his destiny and so to become himself.

"But might alone is the creed of the Great Han Khan. So what for a world that can boast of only its strength and sets but this single gift above all else? Nothing but the folly of this arrogance, I say: that any man should spurn the gifts of the Stars and decide for himself of which he has need and of which he has not. But that you may judge for yourselves for I have no fear of your conclusion.

"Aye, listen to your hearts and you will always know the truth. For by the Stars that shine above the Great Earth and grant to men the gifts they use to make their lives and their world; the truth is set within us all."

"Now listen well and I will tell you some of this truth as I know it to be:

"As for profit: it is good to take pleasure and use from your possessions for they are the reward of your labour. But do not value such things above the gifts of the Stars, nor above the lives of others. For all things are achieved by men with these gifts and can be achieved again so long as the gifts are kept. The beauty of a diamond may be admired, but do not forget that a thousand such will never make a single human thought; or that the value of human compassion cannot be weighed in gold.

"As for the might of a king: what fleeting glory to vainly profit by the subjugation of others and lay up in useless comfort and luxury what could otherwise be used to build a better world? For it is not for nothing that death awaits us all, but it serves that we must ask ourselves this question: what will we leave behind?

"As to the Great Earth Beneath the Stars: this duty we have, each and every one of us, to journey upon the open steppe and sleep beneath the Stars whenever we have need to know their gifts. To go to the desert when our lives are troubled and there, in the silence, to listen to our own hearts tell us what is right and what is wrong.

"As for learning and as for knowledge: all the great measure of this wealth that men have left to us from all the history of mankind is the inheritance of us all. And all knowledge is worthy of recognition, even if it proves not true. For every mistake unveiled brings us one step closer to the truth. Set it only to the judgement of your heart and all knowledge will serve you well.

"As for myself: I speak to you with no more authority than any other man, save for this – that I have walked upon the Great Earth and slept beneath the Stars and I have listened to all that they said."

When Thirsty Horse had finished his speech he stood down from the cart and began to walk slowly and silently through the crowd. Everyone moved aside and they left him pass, while a single child ran forth with the pieces of his guitar and placed them in his hands. Then the silence of the crowd was replaced by the cautious murmuring of the many who had listened to every word that Thirsty Horse had said and who had felt the meaning of those words stir within their hearts.

...

Thirsty Horse continued walking from the Great Ger and the people left him pass since they could see that that was his desire and that his destiny called him elsewhere, just as he had said. He walked on and on until he reached the edge of the camp, and it was not until then that he saw the Great Han Khan's one thousand horsemen – the best of his army, handpicked and loyal to a man, assembled before him to block his way.

So Thirsty Horse stopped and stood his ground, unable to go any further; and he wondered what would happen next.

Then a single horseman rode up to him and dismounted, while all behind him were silent as the man spoke, "Thirsty Horse." he began. "We have no need of war nor of a great khan who will lead us to it. But you who have come from nowhere and announce yourself with no greater pride than the strange name that you bear, will you not lead us? For it is clear that you would bring us to peace with our neighbours and to prosperity: to a fitting challenge for our strengths and our gifts as men, and to honour and dignity above all.

"Oh Thirsty Horse," the man implored. "We ask that you lead us, and will you not accept?"

Now it was such a great honour to be offered this role that Thirsty Horse did indeed consider it very seriously before he replied. But still he replied, "No - much as I am tempted by your offer I must refuse. But although I leave, I have no more fear for your future for I see that now you have set yourselves free from tyranny – and that, I can say, is a decision that comes from knowing in your hearts the secret of life, as I do now in mine. So I thank you again for the honour that you do me, but still my answer is no. You must choose from amongst yourselves a leader who is wise and listen to what he says. Follow him as you must, but not blindly, and do not make of him a great khan. This world has greater need of men who stand as equals together, knowing in their hearts all of the gifts of the Stars, and striving only for the best of themselves and the benefit of all.

But then Thirsty Horse's voice took on a strangely crisp edge as something occurred to him that even he did not expect, and he said, "There is one thing, though, that I would ask of you, and it is this: that even though you will surely depose your King, you continue to treat him with respect and to value his worth. He ruled you harshly it is true, yet he was still the king that you brought upon yourselves and he ruled you as he found you to be. While now that I see him humbled, it is the gift of compassion that settles within my heart."

Then he smiled and his voice became as before, as he concluded,

"As for my own destiny, that I know now in these words that come back to me from my past,

> *'How many stars in the sky and how many people*
> *upon the earth must it take,*
> *Before Man will build a school in which to teach,*
> *Not just some, but all of his children?'*

"That is all and now I have my tryst to keep, for which I am already short of time. So I wish you all success and happiness, my freinds, in the life that awaits you. But you must excuse meand leave me to hurry on my way."

At the end of this second speech of the day, Thirsty Horse raised his hand high in a great salute to all before him, and all saluted him back. Then as he watched, the horses before him began to move, until a great way was cleared for him to walk through, which he did with dignity and a slow measured pace. As he walked a great roaring and cheering went up from both sides of him and his heart stirred to the sound, while he could not help the tears from falling from his eyes.

...

That is the story of how Thirsty Horse left the camp of the Great Han Khan, and it is told for what it says of the hearts of men. It tells of how they do not so often listen to the Stars that shine above the Great Earth and what they say, but more frequently are changed, and that for good or bad, by no more than how they are led to be - by one of their own.

...

202

Chapter 11:
The Journey Back.

With the steady fall of his footsteps upon the ground while he walked, the ger camp of the Great Han Khan faded quickly into the history of Thirsty Horse and became no more than a time that he knew to be over. So he set the memories of that time in their proper place within his mind and his heart, and followed the road that beckoned him on. Although in truth it wasn't quite as easy as that since his body still ached rather badly from the rough treatment that he had received at the hands of the guards. Still, the days of his journey passed to the beat of his relaxed but relentless pace. While since it was a journey that proposed no more strange terrain and no more undiscovered lands, it was a far easier undertaking for Thirsty Horse than had been the journey forth.

Since, too, he had no more desire for adventure left in him, this easy journey and freedom from trouble was all that he even wished for; and now he could pursue his thoughts and reach his conclusions about all that he had lived through. He recognised within himself that he already knew the answer to the question, "What is the secret of life?" Yet still he lacked the words to express it clearly enough for his satisfaction. Consequently, he was always deep in concentration upon their formulation while he walked - and that was a good thing in other ways too, being a distraction that helped him most effectively to forget the aches and pains that remained within his body.

It would take three months to make the journey back and during all of this time Thirsty Horse would not play upon his guitar, not even once, since it remained no more than a collection of sad and broken pieces within his sack. Yet if Thirsty Horse could no longer play for his supper, still his supper had sometimes to be earned one way or another if he were to repay the hospitality of his occasional hosts.

The Thirsty Horse of Mongolia

It was fortunate, therefore, that Thirsty Horse was not completely dependent upon his music in this respect. During his travels he had on several occasions passed for very long periods of time without meeting another human soul – and that had served to teach him well enough how to live off the land. Of course the diet that this led him to was simple to say the least. While on the other hand when he did, from time to time, come within the presence of a culinary delight which could boast the sophistication of, say – a piece of bread, then he was grateful, too, for the pleasure of finding someone to break his bread with.

The absence of his guitar obliged Thirsty Horse to review the options which remained open to him in other respects too, and these are what he considered them to be: He could work for his hosts, should they have work for him to do. He could beg! Or he could use his imagination to come up with a new way of selling his artistic talents - and so that is what he decided to do. The formula that he eventually decided upon to fulfil this new intention was not really so different from the playing of music, however. For to the people he met along the way he told stories instead for their amusement.

Since his repertoire of stories was now very full and since, also, he had discovered that he had the same gift for their telling as he had for the playing of music, he told his stories very well and found the experience to be both as satisfying as it was appreciated. The conclusion being, of course, that when he did meet people along the way he ate as well as he should. But perhaps the greatest pleasure, finally, for Thirsty Horse, was simply to so triumph from his adversity as to see it turned to such useful advantage as this.

Now even just to think like this at the end of such adversity is an admirable achievement in itself. Yet such was the spirit of Thirsty Horse that even then he was not finished from milking all the benefit that he could from his deprivations. There was a delight, too, he

found, in the rediscovery of simple satisfactions in place of the deeds and words of greatness that he had been brought to discover within himself by recent events. Although he could not forget those heights of achievement to which he had risen, of course, and neither would he have wanted too. For no matter how high he had risen, he realised, he had risen no higher than himself.

As for the aches and pains that he still felt from the multitude of bruises that covered his body, he travelled slowly enough to give his muscles time to recover; and he ate as much as he possibly could to give himself the strength to heal. For bruises apart, he had indeed pushed his body to its limits and grown extremely strong in consequence. Yet there comes a time, all the same, when the body can take no more and if it is to grow stronger still, will do so by doing less for a while rather than by doing more.

...

So Thirsty Horse made his way, slowly and patiently, thoughtfully and uneventfully, towards the north-east and towards his tryst with the Cup of Curiosity; and he was very pleased that nothing of note or interest ever did happen to him upon this part of his journey. Not, that is, until after nearly three months of walking and when he was, in fact, not so far from his destination. For it was then, and to his great surprise, that he came across a man who he had met before! None other, in fact, than the man in the strangely coloured robe that he had once passed such an interesting conversation with in the town of his school on the edge of the steppe.

"Hail Thirsty Horse!" cried the still strangely clad figure with obvious delight. "Hail and welcome. I have been waiting here for you quite some time and hoping that fate would bring our paths to cross once more. It is indeed a pleasure that now it has."

"Indeed Sir!" replied Thirsty Horse. "Then I am most honoured that you should think so highly of me and it is certainly a pleasure for me too to meet with you again. But tell me, please, what is it that spurs you to such attentive patience on my behalf?"

"If you do not know," replied the man, "then you do not remember, Thirsty Horse, the words of parting that I left you with when last we met – and can that really be so?" Then the man spoke to remind Thirsty Horse of what he had said before, and repeated almost word for word, "'You have a gift indeed, Thirsty Horse, to see and to understand what you see, and your gift is far greater than I had thought. Your gift is your destiny and it leads you to your future, although you know it not yet yourself. But I know, and I will say no more to you but rather leave your gift to teach you as it will. All that I would wish for myself is that we meet again when you have travelled a little further along the path of your life, and that we may talk then of what you have learned.'

"But now you have passed through that future, Thirsty Horse," added the man in the long and colourful robes, "so I believe that now you may tell me, if you will, of all that it had to tell you."

"Ah" said Thirsty Horse, and then he remembered very well the conversation that he had had with the man before. So he sat with the man a long while and recited the tale of his adventures as the man had asked. The whole story of his adventures, that is, from the day he had left the town of his school, through the culmination of his destiny in the ger camp of the Great Han Khan, and just until this day now. While the man in the long and colourful robe sat and listened in silence and rapt attention to everything that Thirsty Horse said; except for sometimes when he would ask a question if he wished.

When Thirsty Horse had finished the man said, "The tale that you tell is fascinating indeed, Thirsty Horse. And it is most fascinating because for all of time men have tried to understand their origins and their destiny; and by that to know whether their lives are guided by pure chance - or by something greater. Yet very few indeed have ever appreciated so intuitively as you the mysteries of which we speak, nor ever spoken of them so well. Indeed, a new dimension of understanding has been added by your voice, Thirsty Horse. Or at least so it seems to me, who has taken the time to listen."

"Yet for all my satisfaction with your answers, Thirsty Horse," continued the man, "I would ask you one more question still, if you will allow?"

"Most certainly." replied Thirsty Horse.

"Very well then." continued the other. "Then I would ask you this. You have explained these mysteries to me as if their existence had been easy to understand all along – and can that really be so? For consider again what you have said. All is explained in terms of the stars and what they teach, yet what are the stars to teach anything to man?"

Then Thirsty Horse understood for the first time in his life that there was a question here to be answered, and so just as the man had asked he set himself to answer it as best he could, "Before this moment when you put this question in my mind," he replied, "I simply followed my destiny to journey across the Great Earth, and I listened to everything that came to my heart while I travelled. Yet to what it was that I listened, my friend – that I never felt the need to ask."

"But you ask me now;" he continued, "and when I think of it, the stars are of no sort that would ever voice their thoughts to man, for I have learned of them in school and I know what they are as well as I may. Yet still, when I sit at night upon the open steppe and the truth of life comes into my heart, then I look up and see the stars. So although I do not really know what it is that speaks to my heart, yet I see the miracle of the stars and they, as I do know from school, are the greatest of all miracles that this universe can boast - greater a million times over than even the Great Earth herself. So whatever power it is that speaks, what better symbol could there be for it than the stars? But I do not feel that it matters whether I know or not who speaks. Rather it seems to me that it matters only that I listen, and if my simple mind has need to find some symbol for the voice, then for that the Stars will do very well indeed."

Then the man in the strangely coloured robe added after the words of Thirsty Horse these sentences of his own, "A truth remains a truth whether one is taught it or perceives it for one self. While for myself, and after all that I have learned in my long life, I can find nothing in what you say with which to disagree."

Then finally the man asked him, "Now all of this that you have told me, Thirsty Horse. It is the answer to your question, is it not. It is indeed the secret of life?"

Then Thirsty Horse looked very seriously at the man and replied, "Now I understand that the secret of life is the quest of all humanity and each and every one of us has his contribution to make to the composition of the answer complete. While the only thing that is always true is that each of us must make his contribution in his own way, and for that he must first follow freely his destiny and find himself. As to what each of us leaves behind at the end of his life's quest, that is the inheritance of all who follow. Now to serve the Cup of Curiosity I will offer the answer which is, in my own heart, the most meaningful tenet from all the truth that I have learned in all the journeys that I have made."

"Then will you tell me what that is?" asked the man in the strangely coloured robe with just a little hesitation.

209

"Certainly." replied Thirsty Horse with no hesitation at all on his part. Then he told the man the secret of life.

On hearing the explanation the man thought about it for a few moments and then said simply, "Yes, Thirsty Horse. I believe that you are right."

"From all my travels and all my adventures and all my observations of humanity," confirmed Thirsty Horse, "I believe this to be what men most need to learn and so this is the answer that I will give."

They spoke for a little longer, Thirsty Horse and the man in the long and colourful robe, and they discussed together the implications of the secret of life as much as they would, before both were ready to depart. Then Thirsty Horse continued on with his journey of return to the Cup of Curiosity. While the other continued on his way; and without saying as much, retraced the foot steps of Thirsty Horse back to the lands from whence he had come. Because he had found suddenly within his heart that that is what he most wanted to do.

...

When Thirsty Horse finally arrived back at the town of his school on the edge of the steppe, the first thing he did was to seek out Music Maker and to present him with the sad remains of his smashed guitar. For it was that which played most upon his mind.

As for Music Maker, he was so shocked when he saw the ruins of the once beautiful instrument that he jumped back aghast at the sight. Then once he had recovered he offered sadly, "I can give you a new guitar, Thirsty Horse. But it would be a pity to do so, for this one was indeed my best."

Then after Music Maker had thought for a while he said, "Leave it with me until tomorrow and I will see what I can do."

So that is what Thirsty Horse did.

When Thirsty Horse came the next day he was incredulous to see that the guitar had been completely repaired! And although the repairs were plain to see, the appearance of the instrument gave to it now a character that it had not possessed before. Then Music Maker put new strings upon the instrument and tuned it carefully, while Thirsty Horse noted with surprise and delight the sweetness of the tones that sounded as he did. Although whether it sounded even sweeter now than it had before, or whether it was simply that he had forgotten the sweetness of its sound, he did not know.

When the instrument was ready, Music Maker presented it to Thirsty Horse. Then Thirsty Horse sat down and began, quite nervously in fact, to play the guitar again for the first time since it had been broken; and as the music sounded forth as clear and beautiful as ever it had before, he began to cry. As for why he cried there is no need of explanation here, for the reason is obvious to all.

Thirsty Horse played for quite a while just to hear the sound of the guitar, but then an idea occurred to him. So he played through the long piece of music that he had composed himself while he camped upon the steppe between the Khangai and the Gobi Mountains. He played it through without a break and as well as he could - and it was left to Music Maker, the first ever to hear this music played apart from Thirsty Horse himself that is, to tell him that the music he played was beautiful indeed.

"Thank you." said Thirsty Horse to Music Maker when he had finished playing. "Thank you for your compliment and for your sincerity – and thank you for your work. Only now do I feel my life to be in balance again and I myself ready to continue on my way." Then Thirsty Horse stopped playing and stood up to take his leave.

"Wait." said Music Maker. "Do not go yet, Thirsty Horse. Stay the night and let us play together, now that you have your guitar again. I will play upon your own morin khuur that I have always kept here safe for your return."

Of course Thirsty Horse readily agreed to this welcome invitation and so the two of them played together for many hours and deep into the night. When they had finished playing Thirsty Horse said, "All of this that you have done for me I have never paid you for at all. Yet you have a living to earn, Music Maker, and it is not fair that I take so much for free. So tell me how much I must pay you and I will play for the money before I leave the town."

But Music Maker would have nothing of this deal and replied, "Thirsty Horse. I can see that you love the guitar that I made, and you play it better than anyone else. So if you continue to play it always and mention only my name as its maker from time to time then my fortune is assured and you have no need to pay me any more than that."

Which was such a satisfactory arrangement that Thirsty Horse accepted it immediately.

...

It was very early in the morning of the next day when Thirsty Horse set out from the door of Music Maker's ger in the direction of his old school. Although since it was then the period of the summer break and the school would be closed, his hope and expectation was to find his teacher seated once more upon the bench where they had first met - and as luck would have it, so he was.

Thirsty Horse's teacher looked up from his thoughts and saw walking towards him a figure that was not quite the same as he remembered, but that he thought he recognised all the same: the figure of someone of whom he had dreamed so many times. A tall, strong boy, quite a bit heavier and better muscled than he had been before, and who seemed a lot tougher even at this first sight than any boy of only seventeen years had any right to be. Yet could it be who he thought it was? Then the teacher saw that beneath the ravages of experience that duly marked their place upon the brow of this figure there was still a smile of innocence upon his face; and he knew immediately that here at last and once again - was his old pupil Thirsty Horse. Then just as his pupil had done so many times before, and even though he had never in all his adult life been known to be so emotional himself – he burst into uncontrollable tears of happiness!

So great was the joy within his heart as he saw his old pupil come walking towards him, in fact, that he jumped to his feet and ran to greet him with a hug. Then the teacher bade Thirsty Horse to tell all – absolutely all, of the tale of his journeys these past three years. And of course Thirsty Horse accepted so to do.

Now even after all the times that had passed and all that he had seen and done, this was the moment of greatest pleasure that Thirsty Horse had ever known. To meet again with his teacher, whom he loved and respected so very much; and to share with him his experiences and the knowledge he had gained. So Thirsty Horse told his story all over again, and even though it took many hours to tell in all its details and yet many hours more of the next day to discuss, he enjoyed it very much in this telling. Once he had finished the story he offered a compliment to his teacher that was well received and very much appreciated indeed. For he said, "Whatever I have achieved in all my travels, teacher, the greatest debt I owe for that accomplishment is to you. Because you it was who taught me this:

that the greatest part of education is not at all in the knowledge that is learned, but rather it is the training that is given in the use of the mind. By that, it was, that you prepared me more than any other to face the challenges that I found, and to achieve all that now I may count as done."

...

Chapter 12:
The Secret of life

It was once again a beautiful summer's day and all was still and calm in the warm air when finally Thirsty Horse prepared to leave the town and retrace his steps upon the last stage of his journey. Then he struck out for the ger camp where it had all begun, five long years ago. When the Cup of Curiosity had changed a horse into a boy and set him upon a quest to find the secret of life.

After all the journeys that he had now made upon the Great Earth it was a stage, too, that could be quickly and easily passed. So he did not hurry, for he had no need, but only kept a measured pace and declined, this time, to stop for very long at any point along the way. While as to the stars that shone above the open steppe at night, he was happy to sleep beneath them and know again within his heart the creed that they had first taught him all that time ago.

After seven days of walking and just as the light was failing at the end of the day, Thirsty Horse caught his first sight of his destination, and it was the silhouette of the gers upon the horizon that he saw. Then he remembered so very clearly his thoughts of five years ago and he smiled at himself. For the Big Round Things upon the Ground with Smoke coming out of their Tops no longer held for him the mystery that they had – when he had been a horse.

An hour later still and Thirsty Horse arrived at the border of the ger camp itself with the sun finally set and a full moon risen to take its place in the night sky - just as before. As he stood now upon the threshold of his return, Thirsty Horse listened for a while to the bleating of the goats as it came to him upon the cool evening air from their enclosure made of wood. Then he heard the sweet resonance of music as someone began to play upon a morin khuur – and at this his heart leapt! For he knew it to be Ertenbaatar, his friend and first teacher, for sure.

On arriving before the door of the ger that he remembered so well, Thirsty Horse stood still for a moment and listened to the "strange sound of a river" coming from within. Then so much did this sound take him back to his past, that for an instant he thought to rear up on his hind legs and smash down the now repaired door just he had before. But then he remembered suddenly that he was no longer a horse; and it surprised him very much that even after all these five years he had for that moment so easily forgotten this fact.

...

Inside the ger, Thirsty Horse did indeed find Ertenbaatar. Then once again he was obliged to tell the whole story of his adventures, although he told it rather more quickly this time. Not so much because he was tired of telling it, though. But rather because he was impatient to live out his longest held dream: the greatest pleasure that he still kept unrealised within his anticipation – and that was to play music in this ger once again with his friend.

So Thirsty Horse took his guitar, while Ertenbaatar took his morin khuur, and then the two played and sang together for as long as they would. Such was the celebration that resulted that there was no single inhabitant of the ger camp who did not attend that night from the oldest to the youngest child; and of course – I was there as well and witnessed it all.

For several hours the party continued, well into the night, and no one of the revellers, save for Thirsty Horse and myself, and Ertenbaatar of course, knew or probably even cared about the Cup of Curiosity or the tryst. So how, I wondered, would this meeting, which surely must be solemn enough for a magic cup and a "horse become a boy" to discuss the secret of life itself - ever take place?

Yet I should not have worried, for the magic of the hour had no such concerns. I do not remember how it happened; and it seems, indeed, as if I dreamed. But there came a time at the end of that evening when everyone there, save the three of us, had simply fallen asleep and all within the ger was quiet and calm.

Slowly, then, I looked around the place; expecting to find some reason for this change, although what I did not know. So whether I was surprised or not I don't remember now. But soon my eyes fell upon a simple wooden cup that was placed upon a table. It was placed where all could see it, and yet strangely no one had noticed it before and certainly not I. Quickly then I shot a glance at Thirsty Horse and saw that he too was looking silently towards the cup, and so it was confirmed what I already knew for sure – that here was the Cup of Curiosity itself!

And then, of course, the Cup of Curiosity – spoke!

"So, Thirsty Horse. Five years it has been while you have travelled and I have waited. I congratulate you that at least you have survived your adventures. But now - can you tell me the answer to my question so that I will make of you a man? Can you tell me the secret of life? Or will you again become a horse?"

For a moment, then, there was such a total silence between the two that I honestly could have believed that if Thirsty Horse did not answer, then surely it was because the world had come to an end! But then Thirsty Horse did answer; and when he spoke - time began again.

"The secret of life," he began, "is a question that must be answered, piece by piece, by each and every one of us according to himself. To answer the question completely is the destiny of all mankind and its final fulfilment will mark the end of our time upon the Great Earth. But until that day arrives, each must play his part and offer whatever contribution he has to give."

Then Thirsty Horse said, "As for myself, the secret of life that I have learned and offer now is very simple indeed. Yet I offer it still, because after all my travels and all that I have seen and heard and done, this is the secret of life which I have found to be most needed within the hearts of men."

Then Thirsty Horse paused for a few moments while I waited with breath held and heart still - before he said, "The secret of life is simply this, that whoever in your heart you truly believe yourself to be, whether it is a horse, or an eagle, or a wolf, or a man; and if a man then whether a beggar or a soldier, a coward or a hero - then that is who you are. And this I know with certainty, Cup. For in my heart I believe it to be so."

Of course there was a dreadful pause after Thirsty Horse had spoken. But then the Cup of Curiosity replied, "In all that you have said, Thirsty Horse - you are right. For all of that is indeed the secret of life."

Now I do not believe that the boy had ever doubted even for one instant that his answer was correct. Yet still I saw his relief that the Cup of Curiosity had confirmed that it was so.

Then the Cup of Curiosity said, "This is the end for you, Thirsty Horse, of your time as a boy, and from this moment on you will be a man - as is your right and your reward."

While all that Thirsty Horse said in return, and all indeed that was really necessary, was, "Thank you."

"Yet there is still one thing left to discuss," added the Cup of Curiosity, "and that is the last wish. For you have one wish left to use and you must tell me what you would like to do with it."

Then Thirsty Horse thought for quite a long while before he said, "You know, Cup, I would like the wish to be thrown into the air so that it will be taken by all the winds of the Great Earth and spread, like a magic dust, to everywhere beneath the Stars. A little of the magic to fall equally upon everyone and everything, no matter how small the magic will become."

"As you ask," replied the cup, "then so it will be."

Then by some means of magic that I certainly do not understand, I saw within the air before the cup something very beautiful and sparkling but too bright for my eyes to look upon closely and I knew that this was the last wish! Fascinated, I continued to watch as best I could, until suddenly the wish rose upwards and scattered into a wondrous shower of brilliant light. Then the light faded quickly and the shower became a fine golden dust that disappeared through the walls of the ger and I heard a soft sighing of the wind outside. So I can only believe that the dust was scattered to everywhere beneath the stars. A little of the magic to fall equally upon everyone and everything - just as Thirsty Horse had asked.

As for its benefit, though, I do not think that was so small. For it takes a great deal of magic to turn a boy into a horse and then back into a boy again. So I believe, at least, that with this gift of Thirsty Horse, all the world is now a better place.

. . .

Last Words

Now the story ends, and it has been my privilege to write it down, just as I heard it told from my pupil and great friend Thirsty Horse and from others too that I met upon my own journey. For perhaps you have guessed by now, but I will tell you anyway, that I was Thirsty Horse's teacher while he attended my school on the edge of the steppe. Once I had heard his tale in full, I could not help my feet but took leave from the normal duties of my life and went with him to his meeting with the Cup of Curiosity, which it would have been more than my heart could bear to miss. As to all that was said between the two, I have written it down in these pages exactly as I heard it with my own ears. After that I followed my heart again and retraced the footsteps of Thirsty Horse all the way to the ger camp of the Great Han Khan. There I met the monk of whom twice this story tells, and we together it was who finished the telling of this tale.

Yet since it is I who wrote it down there is one last task which falls to me now as a great honour and privilege to perform, and that is to choose the last words to close the book. So here they are for you to read, and my blessing upon you goes with them.

This is a story that belongs to us all, for all to read and take whatever benefit they can from its lessons of the secret of life. For by that you will take what is yours by right of the request of Thirsty Horse to the Cup of Curiosity, and a little of the magic dust of the last wish you will feel - as it settles upon your head.

The End

THE INSPIRATION FOR THE THIRSTY HORSE

Behind these words is where it all began: Sukhbaatar Square, Ulaan Baatar, in January of 2001.

From Ulaan Baatar I took the road to the Terelj National Park with the intention of doing some skiing, some climbing, and of making a film of the adventure.

It was a very cold winter that year, even for Mongolia. Temperatures from a maximum of - 25 during the day down to -50 at night accentuated the bleak austerity of the imagery and emphasised the essential remoteness of the country. Yet the scenes I pictured and the faces of the few people passing by also brought a message, a certain fabulously enigmatic aphorism in fact, very clearly to my mind.

In May of 2002 I took the plane to Hovd, where I met Zoric and Ot and discovered the Altai Mountains and their peoples as I have related in the introduction to this book. Still in love with the region, I was back in Hovd in December of 2002 with a whole team, including one Mongolian and two French professional mountaineers. This time we took two jeeps, actually climbed Mount Tsambagarav, visited again the little town of Erden Boren, and journeyed a lot further into the Altai range. My warmest thanks go to the Mongolian and Kazak peoples in whose homes we stayed, for their hospitallity, and for the chance to share our lives with them, as they with us.

Back in Ulaan Baatar, I contributed to the National Children's Committee the money from my film "No Fear of Wolves" on my return from the first Hovd trip; and by then the Thirsty Horse was kicking strongly in my mind. With the help of my friends I launched the national art competition in November 2002 and on 28th March 2003, organised a small ceremony in the Ulaan Baatar Hotel to announce the winners.

It is two years now since the first of these photographs were taken and in all that relatively short time UB has been developing at a furious pace with everybody rushing to take his part in the new prosperity. Of course I agree with the development, for that is certainly part of the journey, and who of us wishes to be poor? Yet whatever the benefit of riches, there is still that one message in my mind to which money will never reply. For it is, indeed, easier for a camel to pass through the eye of a needle - than for a rich man to enter the kingdom of heaven.

225

"The Road to the Terelj
from Ulaan Baatar"
Mongolia

"Ger with a Pretty Door"
Terelj National Park

"View from the Mountains"
Terelj National Park

"The Accordeonist"
Ulaan Baatar

"The Bus Stop Crowd"
Ulaan Baatar

"Paradise" in the Palace of Culture, Ulaan Baatar

HOVD

My plan for the western region was to make it to Mount Tsambagarav and see if it could be skied. As to how I would achieve this, exactly - for the most part I had to trust to my luck . . .

Please note: some of the photographs in this section are reproduced from video tape and do not have the image quality of still photography.

233

SCENES
FROM THE
NORTH
WESTERN
REACHES
OF THE
GOBI
DESERT

AND BEYOND . . .

This mountain, adjacent to Mount Tsambagarav, is marked on the map as 3,900 m high.

It took two days in the jeep just to get this close; and unfortunately I didn't have either the time to the organisation necessary to try for the summit.

Not wishing to completely abandon my skiing intentions though, I did at least climb high enough to get into the snow on the very top of one of the foot hills and take these photographs. (Sorry about the Gobi Desert dust that got on the main picture negative!)

ERDEN BOREN

Smoke rises above Erden Boren, last town in the North-Western Gobi before you enter the Altai. The people were lovely and the hotel, a large ger, was free - although also unattended. Behind the brown hills, the snow covered Mt. Tsambagarav rises in presence and in spirit.

MOUNT TSAMBAGARAV
DECEMBER 2002

We awoke at 4:00 a.m. and were treated to breakfast and Mongolian salt tea by our excellent hostess.

An hour later we were ready for the mountain. Outside the ger, in the minus twenty centigrade darkness of the night, the desert calm was disturbed by the roar of the blowlamps that our drivers had placed under the jeep sumps to warm the oil before starting the engines. As we drove away, huge Bactrian camels dodged from our headlamp beams on the track before us.

We followed our chosen gully until the ice stopped the jeeps and then began to walk. An hour later the sun began to rise above the great expanse of the Gobi Desert behind us.

At midday, Richard told us straight that we weren't making enough progress to reach the summit together. So I left our two guides to go ahead at their own fast pace.

To be honest we didn't lag that much, and I think we could all have made the summit, although only just, because the top of the mountain proved to be a vast ice cap that was almost flat. But with a minus fifty wind howling hard in our faces and our facemasks reduced to useless blocks of ice, we thought better of attempting the long walk to the very top - this time at least.

The day goes to Richard and Lionel, who made it.

(All photos: Richard Maffioli & Lionel Pernollet)

237

"Lady sings the blues - Altai Mountain Style"
(Photo: Lionel Pernollet)

I sat on my bed in the UB Hotel with those first paintings received, and as I regarded each in turn they brought the Thirsty Horse to life before me. Nearly 500 entries were received from 351 young artists from all over Mongolia. Here are some more of those fabulous works.

THE COMPETITION

THE SPIRIT OF THE THIRSTY HORSE

So the book is finished, but the story hardly so. For with this first publication the Thirsty Horse is at last loose in the world.

As for me, the writer, I made a lot of friends through all of this and we have many plans to promote the spirit of the Thirsty Horse.

So the art competition becomes an international festival of competitions and events including writing, art, drama and music. While we are working too to facilitate cheaper access and better possibilities for anyone who wishes to visit Mongolia and enjoy the adventure of this uniquely beautiful and fabled land.

"To walk upon the Great Earth Beneath the Stars in search of the secret of life, and to play music at the end of the day."

That is the spirit of the Thirsty Horse.

Anthony Sansom
Seoul, South Korea
April 30th, 2003

For more information, please
consult our Web Sites:
http//www.thirsty-horse.com
for the Thirsty Horse;
http//www.thirsty-horse-media.com
for this and other publications by
Thirsty Horse LLC.